From Now

Til Forever

Don Horne

Help Publish Me USA

Red Oak, Texas

From Now

Til Forever

Copyright © 2014 by Don Horne

ISBN-13: 978-0692306659
ISBN-10: 069230665X

Help Publish Me USA

Red Oak, Texas 75154

More Books by Don Horne

Little Rock, Arkansas 1940

Austin and James Johnson, sat with their first cousin, Anna Johnson. They had just finished several sets of tennis at the Little Rock Country Club, and they watched the others play from under a large blue umbrella furnished with a blue wooden table and blue chairs. There were several courts at play with mostly young adults. It was hot and close to midday.

"Wow, Anna, you were awesome today! Why you almost won several games from Jimmy and me!"

When Austin laughed, Anna frowned, ran her hand through her short, blonde hair, and replied, "If I had had a woman for a partner instead of a clumsy man I would have beaten you bad!"

"Come on, Jerry Allen is a pretty good tennis player. You are just sore because we won."

"I don't suppose you want to take me on in singles, do you?"

"I don't think so. You think you could probably take me, and truthfully, you might!"

Anna smiled at Austin's attempt to make peace. On her best day and Austin on his worst, she knew he would beat her.

It was a June day in 1940. The heat rose off the green painted asphalt tennis court in waves. Although all were already tan, the heat made the sweat soak their clothes and drip from foreheads and legs. They were dis-cussing where to go and when to get out of the stifling heat.

Austin and Anna were close enough in age to have been in the same high school class. Both had just graduated with honors and Anna was the Valedictorian. Austin's grade point was a minuscule less, which meant he was Salutatorian. Both were on their way to the University of Arkansas in the fall, and Austin was to leave in a few weeks to start football practices.

He had been a state champion quarterback at Little Rock High School. Anna had tried out and won a position as a cheerleader and would go to The University at the same time.

James, his younger brother, was the heir apparent to the quarterback position for the Little Rock High School, and had played backup to Austin for the last two years. The three were very close friends.

"Let's go get a Coke and a hamburger somewhere!" exclaimed Anna. "I want to drive your new car!"

"Now, wait a minute. My mother is not allowed to drive my car."

"Well, I am not your mother!" She giggled a victorious laugh as Austin handed her the keys.

Austin and James looked at one another and just shook their heads as if there was no use in arguing. The truth is, Anna, Austin, and James, when he was old enough, all had a driver's license. In Arkansas, the legal age to drive a car was 14. The legal age to fly an airplane was 16, and all three had their pilot's licenses. Luke and Levi, their dads, had been pilots and instructors since World War I. All had flown solo, and could fly well long before they were of legal age.

Anna met Amelia Earhart in 1936, and was devastated after her apparent death the next year. She had vowed to continue her legacy. Anna had her blonde hair cut short like Amelia. She still had a picture Amelia had signed of her and Anna at an air show in 1936. She wore riding pants more often than dresses unless she was going out. Kathryn Hepburn, the pants dressing movie star, was her new idol.

She was "worshiped from afar" by most of the young men at school and the country club for she could be merciless with her sharp wit and in her criticisms. Still, Anna had more friends that were male than female for she had no time for giggling, frilly dressed girls her own age.

The threesome inserted their wooden tennis racquets into their presses to keep them from warping, picked up their towels and balls, and started toward the shiny, new, black 1940 Ford Deluxe convertible, which was Austin's graduation present from his parents for a job well done.

James had nearly jumped up and down with excitement to inherit his mother's red 1936 Ford convertible, which Austin had been driving before. James was the one which had kept it washed and waxed. While Austin drove their dad's Cadillac on his dates, James was perfectly satisfied to drive the little red Ford roadster.6

Anna and Austin opened the doors, undid the convertible latches on the inside just above the windshield header, and all three helped fold and stow the top. Just as they finished, a duet of very pretty twin girls dressed in tennis outfits from James' high school class walked up to the car. They were twins although one was blonde and one was brunette.

The especially pretty brunette named Payton spoke up in a melodious voice, "Hi Jimmy. Can Mallory and I go with you?"

James looked at Austin and Anna, smiled, and said, "Sure, why not? I had rather drive my own car any-way."

Both girls squeezed into the seat with Payton next to James, who had a big grin. Austin and Anna laughed to see the threesome and knew he was in good hands.

James turned on the key, pushed the dash mounted starter button, and smiled as the engine started almost as quickly as an electric motor. The car barely had 10,000 miles and was in perfect shape. The 1936 Ford had a three-speed shifter in the floor, and as he put the transmission into first gear, he touched Payton's bare knee.

His face reddened as he said quickly, "I am so sorry!"

Both girls laughed and Payton said, "Aw come on, Jimmy. Girls aren't stupid. You did that on purpose!"

James' face got redder. He got tongue-tied trying to apologize, as the girls laughed hard at him. He finally laughed too when he realized the tease.

Once at the drive-in, both boys pulled their cars in under the shade of the overhang. At once, the popular group was surrounded by raucous and loud youths.

"Nice car!" exclaimed the carhop as she skated up to the driver's side. Jill was a year out of high school and knew the threesome very well as she did all of the regulars. She had on a short red skating skirt and a white knit shirt with stripes on the sleeves and collar. There was a patch, which read, "Red's Drive-In."

Reluctant to have to admit it wasn't hers, Anna said, "It actually belongs to Austin, and I had to beat him in tennis to get to drive it."

"Yeah, right. I don't believe that you beat Austin. Now, what can I get for you guys?"

"Two hamburgers and two orders of fries. I want a cherry coke, and he will have a chocolate shake."

The girl looked at Austin, and in a very flirtatious voice said, "Don't you talk?"

"I only get to talk when she stops to take a breath."

Austin and the carhop laughed as Anna frowned at him. The girl smirked at Anna who made a face at her as she skated away laughing.

"You are so mean to me, Austin!"

"I am just trying to keep you humble."

A handsome young man in a white knit shirt and pressed Bermuda shorts separated himself from a group of guys and started walking toward the car.

"Here comes Mr. Cool," grinned Austin.

"Oh great," said Anna, but her smile gave her away. Of all the rich, handsome men in school, Ben Winston was one of the few she would talk to. He amused her because he was so full of himself, and she made fun of him just to belittle him.

"Hi, Benny. I didn't see you on the tennis court this morning."

"Nah, I got up late. I just came by to check out the action and pick up lunch."

Austin smiled to himself. Benjamin Winston the Third did not like to get sweaty or dirty. He looked like he had just stepped out of the bath. No one wore pressed tennis shorts but Benny. His nose in the air posture and arched eyebrows irritated Austin. Just once, he would like to throw him into a mud hole. The thought left a smile on his face as he nodded to him.

"Call me when the burgers come. I am going to check on James."

Austin got out of the car, and before he could walk the few feet to James and the girls, he had a girl on either arm. He looked back at Anna and winked. She smiled and just shook her head. She was proud to know Austin and James were related to her.

Austin invited all the kids at the drive-in to his house to go for a swim in the pool at 6 p.m. He called home and his mother gave her permission. She told him to stop by Tanner's Market on the way home, and she would call in and place an order for the items for the par-ty.

Everyone was excited for the Johnsons lived on 20 acres of manicured landscape with a swimming pool, tennis court, basketball court, and enough room with a backstop to play softball. They had a middle-aged Chinese man and wife,

John and Lydia Wong, to cook and serve.

The big, walled estate was on Cantrell Road overlooking the Arkansas River. The house itself sat well back from the road with a circular drive up front and a six-car garage behind the house. The front drive had a covering in case of inclement weather for visitors to get out of their vehicles.

The huge double doors opened into a tiled foyer with a staircase on either side to the second floor. The ceiling in the foyer was two stories tall. There was a large library on the ground floor as well as a smaller one on the second. The master bedroom was on the second floor as well as an office for Luke to do his architecture business. The small library was next to the bedroom. The house had six bedrooms, six bathrooms, and the pool house had a party room with separate showers and restrooms. It was one of the largest estates in Little Rock.

By 6:30 p.m., the place was full of loud, laughing young people. John Wong and his wife Lydia were hard pressed to keep up with hamburgers and hot dogs for everyone. John and Lydia had been part of the Johnson household for over 15 years. The Johnsons; Luke, Maddie, Austin, and James, treated them like family.

Austin saw what was happening, and put on a chef hat and apron over his swim trunks. He took the spatula out of the hand of a protesting John Wong's hand and said, "You serve this crowd, and I will cook!"

"Thank you, Master Austin. This very big group. Are you sure you know all these people?" His slight accent showed.

Austin laughed, "Probably not, but it doesn't matter. Mom bought enough food for half of Little Rock!"

Luke and Maddie Johnson, Austin and James' parents, came out of the house with a large pushcart full of ice and two wooden, hand cranked, ice cream mixers. A shout went up from the kids and a line formed to crank the handles. Salt was poured over the ice and the handles were being cranked so hard the kids had to be told to slow it down some to let the ice cream harden. Finally, the crank became harder and harder to turn and Luke stopped the young man on the first handle, opened up the container and announced, "It's ready!"

There were shouts and squeals of delight as the ice cream was put into bowls and Maddie and Lydia had cut up bananas and strawberries for toppings to go with the chocolate and caramel syrup flavorings.

Lydia scraped out the containers, went inside, rinsed them out, and refilled them with more ice cream mix. This time she added a bottle of Orange Crush to give the ice cream an orange color and taste. Again, the kids were pressing forward with their bowls and, after two more creamers full, everyone decided they had had enough.

Even after being warned by Maddie to not go in swimming for at least 30 minutes after eating, there were several which jumped into the pool, splashing everyone. Over half of the huge pool was only chest deep and people were enjoying standing and splashing one another. Maddie smiled and shook her head. She knew from her own experienced it was hopeless to remind youngsters to wait. She didn't, and the kids didn't.

The younger kids started to leave by 9 p.m. and by 10 just the older kids were left to sit by the edge of the pool. Most dangled their feet in the water. The conversations ranged from celebrities to sports, and there were concerns about going off to college in the fall when the world looked so unsettled. Germany had already invaded Poland

and everyone questioned how long before they dragged the rest of the world into a war.

Austin and Mallory, and James and Payton, were on one side of the pool while Anna sat on the other be-tween Jerry Allen and Benny Winston. Anna got up just as two muscular football player friends of Austin and James approached.

"Anna!" said Fred, who was the biggest.

"Whut?" answered Anna in a voice full of sarcasm, making everyone laugh.

Somewhat embarrassed, Fred continued. "Mike and I think you need to take a swim."

"It took two of you to arrive at that decision? Does that mean you each have only half a brain? I am on my way to get a Coke. I don't want to get wet again, and, besides, I don't have time to play games with children!"

The group was suddenly quiet for the two boys were several inches taller and several pounds heavier than Anna's five foot five frame.

"Is it going to be a problem with you and James if we throw her in the pool?" asked Fred, looking directly at Austin. He did not want to have to confront the two brothers.

"Listen, Fred, you are the one with the problem if you try to throw her in the pool. She can more than take care of herself, but don't say I didn't warn you."

Fred and Mike smiled at one another as the two approached Anna. Fred put his hand out first as if to grab her, but Anna grabbed his wrist, twisted her body under him, and threw him over her shoulder into the pool.

Mike also made a grab but grasped at air as she neatly sidestepped him, pulled his out stretched arm to-ward her, and with his own momentum yanked him sideways and let him go. He was flailing his arms as he yelled out, and he too went backwards into the pool.

"Now, leave me alone!"

Everyone stared in silent unbelief at the two hapless young men sputtering in the pool. Anna walked the few steps over to the edge of the patio, dipped her hand into the washtub filled with ice and cold drinks, and picked out a bottle of Coca Cola. She pried open the bottle with the opener attached to the tub handle with a string, took a long drink, and looked back at the crowd of kids who were still staring silently with their mouths open.

"Now what? Haven't you ever seen anybody drink a Coke before?"

Austin and James laughed at what had happened, and went around to the edge of the pool to offer their friends assistance in getting out. Afterward, Fred and Mike stood on the edge of the pool as the water dripped from their clothes.

"What happened?" asked Fred. "Where did she learn that stuff?"

"Our main man, John Wong, is a Chinese martial arts expert, and we have all been taking lessons since we could walk. I tried to warn you." Fred knew he had been had and he smiled at Austin. "You could have tried a little bit harder to warn me. She's dangerous!"

Both laughed, and Fred put his head closer to Austin and said just above a whisper, "Do you think she would go out with me?"

Austin's surprise showed as he said, "Now let me understand this. She just threw you in the pool, and you want to ask her out?"

"Yeah," Fred muttered sheepishly, as he shook his head up and down to clear some of the water.

"Tell you what. You ask her out after you apologize, and if she doesn't throw you in the pool again, you have your answer!"

Austin patted him on the shoulder as he handed him a dry towel and said, "Good luck!"

As the group of kids from the party left, Fred hung around Austin and James and finally saw Anna alone. She was helping pick up towels and leftovers from the party. He walked over by her, picked up a pair of towels, handed them to her, and said, "I apologize."

"Why?" smiled Anna. "I am not the one that was in the pool."

He looked down for a moment, and said, "The truth is, I wanted you to notice me."

"Well, I think everyone noticed you," she laughed.

"Would you go out with me?" Fred blurted.

Anna studied him for a moment with her smile mostly vanished, as she questioned to herself if he was kidding or not. What Fred did not know is Anna had already decided back in grade school she liked him. She smiled a small, enigmatic smile, and said, "Yes, Fred, I would like that, but only if we don't go swimming."

"You don't have to worry about that!"

As she escorted him to his car, she put her arm through his. They made a date for the next night to go to the movies to see Gone With The Wind. He was to pick her up early enough to take her out to eat. At the car, he put his arms around her and she smiled at him.

"I suppose I should apologize, Fred. I was a little hard on you."

"It's okay, really. Little things like I need to leave you alone and keep my hands to myself are things I need to know."

She giggled and kissed him quickly on the cheek and whispered, "See you tomorrow!"

Anna stood and waved as Fred drove away in his dad's red, 1940 Chevrolet convertible. His dad owned Tanner's Markets, which were several large grocery stores in Little Rock and North Little Rock.

Austin and James walked up beside Anna, and Austin teased, "Now I know how to pick up girls! I let them throw me in the pool."

Anna smiled. "I thought I was going to have to grab him and throw him in myself to get his attention. I am glad he thought of the idea. I wanted some way to break the ice with him."

All three laughed and James said, "I think you could safely say the ice is broken!"

The three best friends laughed as they walked arm in arm into the house. Maddie watched through the kitchen window and smiled to herself. She remembered a time when she and Luke, and his twin brother, Levi, were just that close back home in Paris, Arkansas. It seemed so long ago at times, and she relived her childhood through the lives of her boys and Anna, which made it seem like just yesterday. She still had a smile as Luke put his arm around her to see why.

"I remember those times too, Maddie.

Anna is just as independent as if she were your own child. If I didn't know better, I would think you had trained her!"

"Well, we do talk a lot about boys and stuff. She needs guidance as you might guess."

Luke shook his head and hugged Maddie to him and said, "I knew it! You have been responsible all along! You took that sweet little girl and turned her into another Maddie. Lord, help us!"

They both still had smiles as the kids came into the kitchen through the patio doors. Seeing their parents smile at them, both boys frowned as if they did not like to be the object of their affection. However, Anna smiled back.

"Is my room ready? I am tired," said Anna.

"You do know this is not where you live," smiled Maddie.

"Really? Then why do you have a bedroom just for me?"

"When you were little, you played so much and so long here at our house you would fall asleep, and it was easier to call your parents and put you to bed than to get in the car and take you the couple of miles to your house."

"Thank you, Aunt Maddie. I have already called home, and I needed to visit with you anyway. Fred Tanner asked me out after I threw him into the pool."

"Men are such weird, simple little creatures, aren't they? When we were kids I used to make Luke chase me, and I would run just fast enough to let him catch me. He never caught on."

Luke put his arm around Maddie again and said, "That is why I was in such good shape for sports. It came from chasing her!"

They all had a good laugh, and Maddie and Anna walked arm in arm up the stairs to go to her bedroom. Lydia Wong came into the room to ask if there was any-thing else they wanted of her and

John, and after being told she and John had done a good job at the party, they smiled, bowed, and went out the door to their quarters in the back.

Later, as Maddie sat at the dressing table and brushed her hair, Luke asked what she and Anna had talked about.

"Oh, it was just girl stuff. Our little Anna has her first crush and her first real date. I am feeling really old at how much she has matured."

"Yeah, I can see what you mean. She is mature like throwing boys into the swimming pool!"

Both laughed for they could remember similar times from their own youth.

"Truth is," smiled Luke. "I bet he knows now to keep his hands to himself!"

Maddie smiled at him in the mirror and said, "Thankfully, they never learn that lesson. She told me she and Fred were to go with Jimmy and Payton to see Gone With The Wind tomorrow night. She was so excited to finally get to go out with him. He had been the only boy she had had a crush on since they were in grade school."

"Well, he must have liked her also to ask her out after she threw him and Mike into the pool."

Maddie and Luke smiled as they both remembered a time when she had hit him in the stomach in Paris in the well house when he had teased her. She had tried to get away and go back to the dance, but he grabbed her and held her off the ground while he kissed her.

"I guess I did not move fast enough that night."

"Maddie, you moved just fast enough for me to catch you! You wanted me to kiss you!"

"I confess. Try it again and this time I won't run," she said as she smiled.

"It still seems as if Anna should be the little blonde 5 year old who chased the tennis balls on the court or the 10 year old who would hit the ball by the hour against the wall. She could beat anybody except Austin among her friends. Turn the light out, Uncle Luke, and come to bed."

The next day was Friday, and Austin, up early as usual, was sitting by the pool with a cup of black coffee. James and Anna usually slept to mid-morning until they were awakened by the smell of coffee and breakfast cooked by John and Lydia.

"Mind if I join you?"

"No, of course not, Dad."

"I am sorry, son. I have taught you a bad habit of getting up early. Your mother would sleep until she starved to death if someone did not wake her!"

They both laughed and Luke admitted, "Okay, maybe it is not that bad. All the sleep she gets is why she is still so beautiful."

It was no secret to anyone who knew the

Johnsons how beautiful Maddie Johnson was compared to any other middle-aged woman in town, including celebrities. Although she secretly colored her hair a little, even the young guys looked as she walked by in town or at the pool. Luke also was still very fit as an ex-boxer and athlete. He worked out regularly at the fitness center in the country club with Austin and James, and he still could more than hold his own at tennis, handball, and golf. At 49 years of age, however, he dreaded turning 50 on August the 5th.

"Hey, I hear James and Anna both have dates tonight, what about you?"

"I guess I am taking Mallory Potter, Payton's twin sister, but she is such a kid."

"She is just a year younger than you, and she is gorgeous! I bet every guy in Little Rock would love to take her out."

Austin smiled and said, "Well, I am actually proud to take her out and to be seen with her. This will be our third date, and I think Mom is already started to plan a wedding!"

They both smiled and shook their heads. Both Maddie and Luke thought Austin was old enough to have a girlfriend. The thought of a girlfriend to Austin was fine, but he wanted to be able to see what the women were like at the University of Arkansas.

The movie, Gone With The Wind, was to begin at six o'clock, and Fred came for Anna at four o'clock, who was still at her aunt and uncle's house. Austin and James were to pick up their dates at the same time, and all three couples were to meet at the Italian restaurant across the street from the new Palace movie theater in downtown Little Rock. They wanted to get there early to sit in the balcony where the ushers with their flashlights did not patrol so much. Couples with children sat on the down-stairs or main floor. It was no secret, but it was an unspoken custom of most classy theaters. The couples also knew a line would start to form about 5 p.m., and they did not want to stand in line very long.

The three couples were almost first in line. As they stepped up to pay, the teenage girl selling tickets smiled at Austin and said, "That will be one dollar apiece."

Austin, who was to pay for everyone, asked, "Why so much? On most Saturdays we can see a double feature and a cartoon for only twenty-five cents!"

"It is a special movie, and it is real long. It even has an intermission. I don't set the prices anyway."

Austin smiled to let her know he was kidding, and she smiled back and said, "You sure are an ornery cuss, aren't you?"

Austin handed her a twenty-dollar bill for everyone's tickets and told her to keep the change. Anna, who knew the girl from school, said into the talk opening of the booth, "Yes, Janie, he is always like that. Don't pay any attention to him." Janie put her head close to Anna and said in a low voice, "I wish he would pay attention to me!"

"I will put in a good word for you."

Both girls smiled at one another as the little group hurried up to the balcony. As soon as the lights went down for the movie to start, everyone took their dates' hands except Austin and Mallory. Anna squeezed Austin's arm, and when he turned to look at her, she looked down at her and Fred's hands and nodded toward Mallory. Austin rolled his eyes and put his hand over his date's hand. She turned and smiled at him, turned her hand over, and started holding his hand. Austin leaned over to Anna and whispered, "Would you quit trying to run my life?"

"You are so dense sometimes, Austin. Someone needs to teach you some etiquette and manners about going out on a date!" she whispered back.

She patted Austin's arm and smiled as she leaned over and put her head on Fred's shoulder who was smiling broadly and thinking to himself it was definitely worth a dip in the pool to be holding Anna Johnson's hand.

After the long movie, all three couples stopped for Cokes at the drive in, and as Austin and James took their dates home, Fred and Anna went to her house.

Levi and Ellen Johnson's home was similar in size and design to Luke and Maddie's, for Luke had drawn the designs and oversaw the construction for both.

Levi and Ellen were sitting and reading in the study as Anna opened the door. Fred held the door open as they entered the foyer. As they entered the room, Levi stood and smiled at the couple. He had known Fred and his dad for years. He extended his hand to Fred and said, "Was it worth a dip in the pool to have a date with Anna?"

Fred, a little embarrassed, looked at Anna.

Anna shrugged her shoulders and said, "I did not tell them. Aunt Maddie told Mom."

Fred nodded and smiled at Anna, "Oh yeah. It was worth it."

Everyone laughed as Anna put her hand in his and rewarded him with a smile.

Ellen had cookies and drinks for the kids, and after serving, she and Levi were getting ready to go upstairs to bed. Anna began showing the house to Fred. As they walked around the study, Anna pointed out pictures and told him about Grandpa August and Molly, who were still pastors of a good-sized church in Paris, Arkansas.

She showed pictures of her dad and Uncle Luke in World War One, and then of the early days in the air mail service. She showed him pictures of the air transport days and then of the pictures when the two couples went to Hollywood at the invitation of Robert Allen, the producer, to fly airplanes for stunts.

"Why, that is Clark Gable standing with your dad and mom, and your aunt and uncle! I recognize several other movie stars as well!"

"It was no big thing. Dad and Uncle Luke flew as stunt pilots in a couple of movies. Although, Aunt Maddie, ALWAYS the daredevil, did do a little wing walking in one."

"Wow! I am impressed! You must get your crazy ways from your Aunt Maddie!"

"I am afraid she does, Fred. I am terribly afraid of heights," smiled Ellen, Anna's mom.

"We are going to be friends then, Mrs. Johnson. I am so afraid of heights I don't even like to ride the Ferris Wheel at the fair!" Everyone laughed.

The Johnsons said good night, and Anna and Fred took their drinks out beside the pool and sat in the double swing on the patio. They had known one another for years, but both were a little shy toward one another as they talked and looked for parameters for their new relationship. Both wondered where they were to go from there.

Anna put her head over on Fred's shoulder as he put his arm around her.

"You know, Fred, this just seems right somehow. I have known you since grade school, but I never dreamed you liked me too."

"Anna, you have thrown me into a swimming pool, and when we were younger you threw sand on me from the playground. You must have liked me a lot for a long time for you to be so mean to me! You must have known I liked you too."

"I guess I did, but I could not get you to do anything about it. So, when the opportunity came, I took matters into my own hands."

Fred kissed her quickly and said softly, "Well, I am glad you did."

"Listen, Anna, would you like to go to the Travelers game tomorrow afternoon? They are playing some team from Texas which is supposed to be pretty good."

"Sure! I have not been this summer. What time are you picking me up?"

"Game starts at one, but let's go early enough to watch batting practice. Say I pick you up at eleven thirty and we can eat something before we go."

"Great. I will be looking forward to it."

The Little Rock Travelers were a minor league baseball team, which played in the old Texas League at Ray Winder Field which was built in 1931. It was a highlight of the summer for nearly everyone both young and old to get to go and experience baseball at its best, complete with hotdogs and the sounds of the fans.

The couple talked and laughed about the pool incident, their friends, and discussed the movie, which was already being banned for having a curse word at the very end. Both Fred and Anna were of the opinion this one word would lead to more foul language in movies.

"I better go, Anna."

Anna walked Fred to his car hand in hand and kissed him as if her mother saw, because she knew she did. It was still enough to make them feel warm, and Anna held him with her head on his chest for a moment be-fore she let him go.

"Good night, Fred. I enjoyed it."

"Me too. Tomorrow cannot get here fast enough!"

Anna's mother smiled at her as she came into the house. Anna hugged her mom and told her, "He is really nice, Mom. He treats me like a queen."

"He knows if he doesn't you will throw him back into the pool!"

The three couples started being seen

together every day in some way. They went to see the Travis baseball team play and went for a swim at Rockaway Beach. Some nights on the weekends, they went to the Asher Drive In Movie, and at least one meal a day was usually spent at Pete's Drive In.

The group was at the drive in under the canopy with Austin, Mallory, Anna, and Fred in Austin's car with the top down. James and Payton were in his car beside them also with the top down. Jill, the blonde, pretty carhop, who flirted with Austin just to irritate Anna, had already brought hamburgers and drinks.

"Austin, when are you headed for the university?" asked Fred. He and Austin were to be roommates.

Anna was glad. It would give her a chance to be around both of her favorite men at the same time. She had been accepted as a cheerleader, and looked forward to campus life.

"We have to be there on Monday the 12th of Au-gust for the start of football two a days. So, I guess I will drive up on Saturday. How about you?"

"Yes, of course. If you want, we can travel together. Anna says she is riding up with me. She has to be there to practice cheerleading."

"Well, if the school would let freshman women have cars on campus the way that guys get to, I could drive myself. I even have to live in the dorm. Not fun. I will probably get some loser for a roomie."

"I feel sorry for who gets you!" kidded Austin.

"Mallory, slap him for me. I can't reach him!" They all laughed.

"Besides, you don't even have a car."

"Well, I intend to look, and take my time. My family has several cars and if I need to borrow one, they are available."

"What would you really like to have?"

Anna looked pensive for a moment as if she wondered should she tell them the truth. She looked at Fred and then Austin.

"Believe it or not, I would like a new Ford Woody Station Wagon. When I went with my folks to New Hampshire last winter to go skiing, the hotel owner picked us up and our luggage in one. It was the neatest thing. Then, when we all went to California last summer, some of the kids were in older woody station wagons to carry their surfing paraphernalia. Okay, you asked, and I told you the truth."

"Anna, I think that would be a perfect car for you, especially as much as you like to camp and picnic with your friends. Don't look at me like that, for once I am being serious with you!"

Anna smiled at him in appreciation.

"Well, we better get home," she said, "We are eating at your house tonight and I want to clean up first. So, if you don't care, Austin, take Fred and me to my house. His car is over there for some reason. My dad is thinking about adding on to the garage to give him a stall of his own." Anna smiled at Fred and patted his knee, when everyone laughed at him.

"We are to eat at six," said Austin, "and you know how John and Lydia like for everyone to be punctual. Sometimes I forget they are not really family, but they are so much a part of the Johnson household they may as well be."

"How did they come to be at your house?" asked Fred.

"It is a long, but great story. I will ask John to tell you sometime."

The meal of fried chicken, rice, egg rolls, and salads was served outside, and afterward everyone was sitting and visiting. John and Lydia joined them after making sure everyone was served. Fred told John he was interested in hearing his life story. John and his wife looked at one another, and Lydia spoke quietly, "It is up to you, but everyone loves to hear it because it shows sometimes God blesses us in unexpected ways."

"Well," said John in a measured voice as if he were picking his words carefully. "You may or may not know China was ruled for centuries by dynasties of emperors and one of the final dynasties was the Xing Dynasty. China at that point was ruled by two women, Empress Dowager Ci'an and Empress Dowager Cixi. The most ambitious was Empress Dowager Cixi. She had been taken to the Emperor's court as a concubine at the age of 15. She passed her audition and was added to the Emperor's harem. She began way down the "pecking order" on the princess line, but by having a son by the then emperor whom she named Tongzhi, she became an empress.

Although he was only half-legitimate, it was enough to ensure her presence in the palace.

He became Emperor at the age of 18, but had been trained since he was 5 years old. However, Tongzhi died without a male heir, which created a crisis in the succession of the dynastic line.

After great disagreement between the two dowagers, they finally agreed upon Zaitian who was the first born of First Prince Chun Yixuan and Cixi's sister. He addressed Ci'an as "Huang O'niang" (Empress Mother) and Cixi as "Qin Baba" or (Biological Dad) to reinforce the image of her as the fatherly power figure.

Empress Ci'an died, after a short illness, of smallpox in April 1881. Ci'an's death meant the balance of power was now in Empress Cixi's favor.

Prince Gong, a warrior prince and once a favorite of Cixi, was a strong leader and struggled to gain more power, but Cixi downgraded his position to "advisor" and promoted the more loyal Chun to President of the Navy and the Army.

Prince Chun, in what looked like a move of great loyalty, took funds from the military and began to reconstruct the Imperial Summer Palace outside of Bei-jing. The invading Russians had burned the palace, and Chun pretended the move was for the retirement of Cixi. Prince Chun in reality did not want Cixi to interfere with the young Guangxu's rule once he became of age.

My father, Langxu, was Chun's second born, and was born just outside Beijing in 1875. As was the custom of the time, lesser-born nobility were sent to America and other countries to study abroad. My father was trained in English and mathematics at Stanford University in California. He met a beautiful San Francisco socialite in college by the name of Louise Hearst who was a distant relative of Randolph Hearst. He wanted to marry her, but to do so meant he had to give up everything in Chinese nobility.

The Empress Dowager Cixi did not really

care if he did because it meant her position and power was even more solid with him removed as a possible threat. In an unprecedented show of generosity, she gave him a wed-ding present of over a million dollars American in cash, plus quite a bit in stocks and bonds.

You can imagine what a 25 year old millionaire acquired in scurrilous friends from the Hearst family and other deceitful people. They lived very well for the time in San Francisco, and then moved to the Los Angeles and notably Monterey, California, area.

My father was very naïve, and lost most of his money by trusting this group of people, which made a living, and their fortunes, from conning and cheating people.

I was born in 1898 and was already in college at UCLA when my mother went back to her people in San Francisco. My father went back to China and was heralded as a long lost son returning from a far country. He was loved and accepted all over again as the brother of the new Emperor. He died a few years later and was given a funeral ceremony as befitted a nobleman. He was buried by the time I found out, and I might not have gone back to China anyway. I already had some money coming in from a trust fund to go to school, plus, I found I loved to cook, and took a part time job in a nice restaurant for extra money. I was only interested in martial arts, which is fairly nonexistent in America, and the job gave me some-thing to do when not in school.

I met Miss Lydia in one of my philosophy classes. We were antagonists at first in most debates. I was from the Chinese culture and was very conservative. She was, and still is, a Progressive or a Socialist. You know the scenario. What started as a war of words, grew into respect, then friendship, and finally I shocked all my friends by asking her to marry me!"

"Well how did you meet Mr. Johnson?"

"He and Miss Maddie loved to come to the up-scale restaurant where I worked, whenever they were in Los Angeles. They kept sending very generous tips back to the Chef, which was me. So, after a few times, when-ever they came to the restaurant, they would ask for me and I would come out personally and take their order. My manager did not mind at all. Luke Johnson tipped and paid very well!"

Everyone smiled and looked at Luke.

"What can I say? He was the best, and still is, chef I have ever met."

Everyone nodded their head and murmured agreement.

"Okay, but how did you become friends?"

"Let me answer this," smiled Luke. "One night Maddie and I had stayed very late visiting with friends and business associates, and the restaurant was already closed by the time we left.

John saw us and waved. We offered him a ride. He started to walk and talk with us on our way to the car. He asked how we liked his signature dish, Beijing Chicken a'la John Wong. We were approached by four men in the empty parking lot.

'Give me all your money, pretty boy!' One of them said. When I said, 'no!' he looked at the others and laughed. 'Well I guess we will just have to take it!'

'You might want to pack a lunch, there are only four of you and there are two of us.'

'I think a pampered Pretty Boy and a little Chinaman we can handle. Besides, I have a knife!' he said, very cocky and self-assured.

'Let's see it,' spoke up John about that time. I thought to myself, 'John stay out of this. I can handle it!'

The guy put out his hand and pushed the button on a switchblade knife. By the time the blade clicked fully open, John had grabbed the man's wrist, twisted it, took the knife away, and elbowed him in the face breaking his front teeth and caused blood to flow everywhere! He was knocked backward from the blow about three paces. He held his hand over his bloody mouth. John whirled around so fast he was a blur, and kicked the man in the chest. He went flying back and was caught in the arms of his three friends. He was out cold! I don't know who was more surprised, the four guys or me! Here stood this little, five-foot-five Chinese Chef, no offense, John, still in his white uniform as he held the man's switchblade and asked if they still wanted our money.

The men picked up their friend and ran away, and looked over their shoulders to make sure he did not follow them! Their eyes were wide open in fear and astonishment! John looked at me, I looked at Maddie, and I looked back at John, and said, 'So, that is what they mean by Kung Fu!'

John quietly bowed a little bow."

John took over the narrative.

"Maddie and Luke gave me a ride back to the nice hotel where Lydia and I lived. I did not have a car or a license, and all the cabs had pretty much quit running by that time at night. Today, they run all the time. Any-way, we sat and visited in the lobby with Lydia, who had come down from our apartment, and we decided to go back to Little Rock together. Lydia could not have kids from a childhood illness, Austin and James were very young, and they needed someone to help take care of this huge house. So, here we are!"

"What a story!" exclaimed Fred. "So, that is where Anna and the guys picked up Kung Fu...from you!"

"Actually, as the son of nobility, I was taught Washu, which is lot more potent form of Kung Fu. I am also expert with sticks and double knives. In Chinese military, the nobility leads the men into battle. We have to know how to protect ourselves."

"I learned my lesson in Washu from Anna!"

Everyone laughed as Fred smiled at Anna.

As the party ended, the Potter sisters, Payton and Mallory, and Fred, now understood why even as "masters of the manor" the children joined in since childhood and helped John and Lydia clean and pick up.

"I am impressed how your folks have taught you how to clean after a meal," said Fred to Anna and Austin. They both laughed out loud.

"John taught us, and mostly by example. We thought if a noble Chinese prince could clean, we could too. We have never questioned the practice. It makes his job easier."

"Your family is special, Anna!" smiled Fred.

Anna walked Fred to his car. At his car,

Fred put his arms around her as she leaned against the driver's side door. The warm Arkansas night surrounded them with the sound of crickets and the flashing of fireflies. Anna put her head on Fred's chest after they kissed and held him tight.

"You smell better, Anna, than honeysuckles and Magnolia blossoms!" He held her to him as he smelled the fragrance of her hair.

"Wow, look at you! My big football player is turning into a romantic! Next thing you will be spouting poetry!"

"I have never felt this way about anyone. For now, would you go steady with me?" He looked into her eyes.

She raised her face up to him and said softly, "We are going steady, Fred. There's no one else for me either."

She kissed him again.

Austin and Mallory went for a drive along the Arkansas River, and parked overlooking the slow moving current.

"I thought you might want to watch the submarine races, Mallory."

Caught off guard for a moment, she squinted her eyes and looked at the river. "What? I don't see anything."

Austin smiled but wanted to see just how far she would go before she caught on. "Look, the red one is get-ting ready to pass the yellow one!"

Mallory looked one more time before Austin burst out laughing.

"Mallory, they are submarines. They are under the water. You can't see them!"

"So you teased me the whole time? I wondered why I couldn't see them!"

Austin by then was nearly hysterical with laughter.

Mallory frowned and said, "Well, I don't think it is that funny!"

"Actually, I just wanted to bring you up

here to go parking."

"Why didn't you just say so? It's okay by me!"

She put her arms around his neck. After a moment of very passionate kisses, he pushed her back and whispered, "Mallory, we can't. I do care for you, but I am going to be leaving in a few days. I am not going to be just a summer lover. Let's just enjoy the moments together, and see how we feel after you go to school for your Senior year."

She looked him in the eyes for a moment. Tears began to form and she stopped and sat upright.

"Thank you, Austin. I am still a virgin but I confess my first time could have been with you tonight."

She kissed him sweetly on the lips and said, "I don't know where she is right now, but there is a woman somewhere that does not know she will meet a dreamboat named Austin Johnson!"

"You know, Mallory, the same goes for you. I am not what you need right now. You need consistency and a long-term relationship, and I just cannot give it to you. Do you understand this is not rejection, but a declaration of how much I care and respect you?"

She shook her head up and down yes. As Austin drove her home with her head on his shoulder, he did not notice the tears.

The Birthday Party

Luke and Levi Johnson's birthday was on Monday, August 5th, in 1940. Because they were to turn 50, Maddie and the family planned to have their huge party at the Little Rock Country Club. What started as a party with just a few close friends, turned into a happening with several movie star friends wanting to attend. Robert Allen and his wife, Lela Mae, also sent word they were coming. With all the celebrities coming, the guest list had swelled to well over three hundred!

Luke took John Wong, Austin, and James with him to purchase each a new tuxedo. Levi met them from his workplace, the Arkansas Gazette Newspaper, where he was the Senior Editor. They went to a small, family specialty-clothing store called Lou Hoffman's. All three men tried on formal wear, and when Luke stood and looked at himself in the three-way mirror, Levi walked up behind him and stood with a smile.

"Do you remember when Pop got married to Molly, and we drove up to Fort Smith to buy all of us new suits? We never saw him laugh and smile as much as we all did on that trip."

"You know, Levi, I am really a private person. These sort of things make me nervous. I wish Maddie and my family would have just given us a private little party."

"Actually, that was the way we started out, but after we invited one friend we could not stop! Who do you not invite? Face it, Luke, you and I have a lot of friends from our glory days at the University of Arkansas, the fighter squadron in World War I, the mail and passenger air lines, the movies, the architect and building business, not to mention the people we have met here at the Country Club.

You are a good, honest family man and businessman, fun to be around, and every one that meets you goes away thinking they are your best friend. Face it, Luke, no one at this party will do anything but wish us the best."

"You're right, I guess. That is why they call you the smart one!"

They both laughed at the old, private joke, and Levi patted Luke on the back.

"There you go, my brother. I am proud to be your brother. Besides, YOUR birthday is MINE!"

They both laughed. Luke said, "See? You really are smarter than me! I forgot we are twins!"

The Country Club had two huge dance floors, and both were filled the night of Levi and Luke's party. The one ballroom inside was filled with more of the older guests there to hear the celebrities sing and dance to the orchestra. The dance floor outside by the huge pool was more youthful in decorations and guests. The loud music, instead of an orchestra, was a "swing band." Inside, while the older folks did the waltz, the guests outside danced the hop and the jitterbug. The distinctive music and festivities between the two dance floors led Levi to make an observation.

"Every generation seems to be defined by their music. It is widening the generation gap even more by polarizing the youth and their music from the older folks and their music."

Maddie stood, and all the men stood also. She smiled at the show of respect. She loved to dance and listen to the music. The table included several celebrities who were friends from her movie days.

"Well, I want to participate, and so, I think I will go out and dance to the band for a while instead of the orchestra." She walked around the table and put out her hand.

"How about you, Mr. Fred Astaire?" asked Mad-die. He was one of the celebrities. "I am not Ginger Rogers, but I am not afraid to try and I love to dance!"

After only a moment or two on the dance floor, the two were alone as Maddie danced with arguably the most influential modern dancer that ever lived. Maddie did very well though the dance steps were kept simple for her. There were lots of whirls and Maddie held Mr. Astaire's hand while he did the showy dance steps. Afterward, he escorted her back to the table, and bowed to her to a thunderous round of applause.

It was a loud, festive affair. With all the celebrities and distinguished guests in attendance, even the radio stations from around the country were present!

Seated at the Guest of Honor table were several celebrities including Clark Gable, Carole Lombard, and others. Maddie got a nice smile and wink from Clark, and lots of eyebrows went up, and Maddie just laughed. She, Clark, and most importantly, Luke, knew they were just friends.

With Levi and several of his reporters present, the Arkansas Gazette carried the account of the party on the front page the next day. It even showed Maddie and Fred Astaire dancing.

Fred Tanner and Anna danced to Duke Ellington. Everyone wanted to see the new dances and new steps. Other "swing bands" included the bands of Glenn Miller, Tommy and Jimmy Dorsey, and even Louis Armstrong stood and played. There was so much laughter, which came from the main ballroom that when the band took a break everyone went inside to listen.

It was a small group of Jewish "Catskill comics" which included George Burns, Rodney Dangerfield, Jack Benny, Don Rickles, and more.

The jokes came one after another as the comedians stood in a line on the platform.

"I just got back from a pleasure trip," said one, "I took my mother-in-law to the airport!"

When the laughter died down enough to hear, another comedian said sadly, "I took my wife to the same hotel where we spent our wedding night. Only this time I stayed in the bathroom and cried!"

"We always hold hands when we go out. If I let go, she shops!"

"She was at the beauty shop for two hours. That was just for the estimate. She got a mudpack and looked great for two days. Then the mud fell off!"

A drunk was in front of the judge. The judge says, "You have been brought here for drinking. The drunk says, "Great, let's get started!"

Each comedian took his turn to amuse the crowd. Even though a lot of greats were present, Luke and Levi still received a tremendous round of applause when introduced as the "Birthday Boys." The cake was six feet tall and lit by 50 candles. Everyone received at least a small piece.

Later, at home with several friends sitting by the pool, Luke stood and clicked a spoon against his water glass.

"One is a very rich man to have this many friends. I thank you from the bottom of my heart for making this a special day. Thanks to my wife and family, I will cherish this memory as long as I live."

Luke sat down quickly, but everyone saw him tear up from emotion. He could no longer speak. He pointed to Levi and nodded for him to say a word. There were several people dabbing at their eyes with handkerchiefs.

Levi stood and in almost a solemn voice looked at Luke and said, "I have always enjoyed being the "lesser" brother. No, I mean it! Luke is one of the finest people I have ever met. His integrity, courage, and intelligence are unlike anyone I know."

Robert Allen laughed, "We are not going to start singing and have a group hug are we?"

They all laughed and gathered around the two men to shake hands and pat them on the back.

Richard Allen and Lela Mae spent the night with Luke and Maddie, and Levi and Ellen joined them as they sat up and talked until the sun just started to lighten the Eastern sky.

"You know, thanks for everything, Richard. Our lives would have been totally different without you. I am proud you are my friend."

Richard stood and shook hands and then hugged him.

"Do you want to go steady?"

They all laughed out loud.

At the airport the next day, everyone shook hands with celebrities as well as family members, which had traveled to the party. The newspaper again reported on the event as well as took dozens of pictures.

Off to College

The trip a week later to Fayetteville and the University of Arkansas was like a family outing. Mallory rode with Austin, and Luke, Maddie, Levi, and Ellen all went in Luke's big Cadillac. James and Payton went in his car, and Anna rode with Fred. Mallory's parents, had told their farewells back in Little Rock, and she and her twin sister, Payton, rode with James.

Once in the dorm, Anna and Austin waited an embarrassing few moments while their mothers made their beds. It was even worse to them when they got ready to leave and their parents gave them hugs and kisses.

"Aw, Mom," whined Austin. "It's not like we are leaving home. We will be home every long holiday and weekend. Besides, if we really had to see you, Dad can come up in our plane."

"Austin, it is not you I am worried about. It

is me missing you!"

Austin put his arms around his mother and held her for a moment while she laid her head on his chest.

"Mom, this should be the best part of your life. It is like making a kite and then see if it is going to fly, and how well is it going to fly."

"You are right, Austin. You are going to do well in life. I am already proud of you, and when it comes James' turn to leave, he will do well too. But, I am a mom and I still hate to let go of my little boys!"

Austin hugged her tight and just shook his head, because he knew she was right, and this was hard on her. He could be embarrassed for her show of affection, but he loved his mother.

Austin, Anna, and Fred stood by the Spoofer's Stone on the quad and watched as everyone loaded and waved goodbye to their family. It was emotional but they were ready to start their college careers.

"Well, needless to say, but you guys did okay on your roommates, but I wonder what I'll get. I saw her name on the door, and she is from Alabama. She must be a cheerleader too to be coming early, but she went to high school in Birmingham at a private school for girls. I am sure she is going to be a snob."

"You are prejudging someone you have never met. You can do better than that, Anna. You are almost a socialist in that you want to have everyone treated fairly and equally," said Fred.

"Fred's right, Anna. Give her the benefit of the doubt. At least wait and meet her."

"Her name is listed on the door as Elizabeth Ann Davis, and in parenthesis is (Beth Ann). Let's go over to the girl's dorm and see if she is here yet."

The threesome walked along the sidewalk and read the names on the bricks. Every year each

Senior had his name put on the walk. It had been going on since 1876.

"Look!" exclaimed Anna, "There's dad and Uncle Luke's names! Class of 1911 for their undergraduate degrees, and Class of 1912 for their Master's! And there is Mom's name, Class of 1912!"

"Wait until you go to the gym and see my dad's name along with your dad's on the trophy for going undefeated in 1909 and winning the conference with a single defeat in 1910! Plus, dad was All Conference in boxing! Seeing all this and knowing they walked this same campus makes me feel right at home! What about you, Fred?"

"My dad came for two years and then went back to Little Rock to help his dad open another grocery store. I am still very proud of him. He and his family own stores all over Little Rock, North Little Rock, and Hot Springs. My dad made it all happen. His dad died not long after he came home, but he had time to teach him the business and he has done well."

Anna put her hand in Fred's, smiled at him, and said, "He did do well!" Then she kissed him quickly on the cheek.

"Public displays of affection are not allowed on campus, young lady!"

All three turned to see a woman dressed in gray and beige clothing. She could have been forty years old, or sixty, or even thirty. She had a very commanding presence with a dour frown on her face. A middle-aged black man, with "salt and pepper" hair in a dark suit, was struggling under a huge armload of suitcases, hatboxes, and vanity cases and was sweating while he stood behind her. A smaller and younger version of the woman with a similar hairdo and colored clothing stood alongside him while the mother had stepped forward to address Anna.

"Or what?" said Anna, and took a step

73

toward her.

Her eyes widened as Austin stepped between the two women. She was not used to people confronting her. He knew the woman at best was going to receive the first and worst tongue lashing she had ever received, and at the worst.....He reviewed what could happen, and was alarmed at the possible havoc an out of control Anna might wreak on her. He tried to diffuse the situation.

"Look, Mam, we have only been here for a few hours. We should have read the part about kissing in public in our handbook. Although I have to admit I have seen others kiss and holding hands too. It obviously offends you and your husband, and we apologize."

The man with the luggage smiled behind her back and then quickly stopped.

"I am not married. This man is not my husband! Did you not notice he is black?"

"That is going on a lot these days. Most people we know are married though."

"You simpleton! This man is my chauffeur!"

"My mistake, mam. I apologize. Excuse us we are on our way to the new Freshman Girl's Dorm to visit my cousin's room." Austin smiled at her for he had been teasing the entire time.

The woman sniffed, put her nose up in the air, turned around, and said sharply, "Samuel, get those bags up to Beth Ann's room and come back and get the others! Now!"

Anna looked at the girl and said, "I don't suppose your last name is anything but Davis, is it?"

The woman spoke again in a very impatient tone, "Yes, it is Davis! Why is that important to you?"

"Well, there is a Beth Ann Davis who was supposed to be coming today. She is a freshman also, and she is from Birmingham, Alabama. We were going to be roommates, but I am sure you can find another room."

"Why should we move?" the woman asked haughtily.

Anna looked the lady in the eyes and said, "First, I am already moved in with the bed made and everything of mine on my half of that room. Second, my clothes are in the closet and put up. I am not going to move, and it is not open for discussion!"

Anna stepped around the woman and looked at the girl who had not said a word yet, smiled a little smile, and said, "She doesn't let you talk much, does she?"

The girl smiled timidly at Anna, glanced at her mother, and said, "I don't have to talk much. She speaks for all of us."

Her mother frowned and started to walk toward the limousine. She looked over her shoulder at her daughter and Anna, stopped, and turned around to face them. She said with a little smile, "I know we do not agree on some things, Beth Ann, and coming all the way to Arkansas when we have great schools in Alabama is your way of getting away from me. However, I do want the best for you. I hope you are happy here."

She walked back toward the girls to within a couple of steps, smiled a surprisingly warm smile at Anna, and said, "You will take good care of my baby girl, will you not? She is all I have." Mrs. Davis stuck out her hand to Anna.

She took her hand, and before the woman could do anything, Anna hugged her briefly.

"We will be okay, Mrs. Davis. I promise. Stay in touch, and do not worry about her."

Tears began to well up in the woman's eyes.

"Thank you, Anna. I am so glad she has found a friend like you, and I know I was somewhat harsh before. I am sorry."

Then, to everyone's amazement, she hugged Beth Ann and pulled Anna to her too! She turned away quickly as if a "public display of affection" embarrassed her. Also, she did not want anyone to see her cry.

She waved from the open window on the limousine as they pulled away from the curb and left Beth Ann's luggage on the sidewalk after being assured the men would take it up.

Fred, Austin, and Anna helped Beth Ann carry her luggage up to her room, and in just a few moments the bed was made and clothes put away. The group was friendly as they worked. Austin mentioned he was hungry and everyone agreed.

"Go with us, Beth Ann. We were just going to eat. I'll even buy!" smiled Austin.

She saw the slight blush on Beth Ann's face, and Anna smiled a little smile.

"My Cuz!" she thought.

By Monday morning, Beth Ann was part of their group. Austin and Beth Ann even held hands in the car as they came home on Sunday evening after church.

The two couples sat in the lobby of the girl's dorm and visited until the lights were dimmed which signaled it was time for all male visitors to leave. This time the guys hugged the girls, and managed a quick peck on the cheek before they left for their own dorm.

The housemother stood with crossed arms and watched. She cleared her throat. Austin winked at her. She actually flushed a little. She was not used to having young men wink at her, especially none with the audacity or good looks of Austin Johnson, but they left quickly. They did not want yet another confrontation over public displays of affection.

After the boys left, Anna and Beth Ann washed their faces and hands, removed what little makeup they wore, and put on their pajamas. They decided to sit up and visit. The first topic was Austin, and was brought up by Beth Ann.

"Austin is quite a guy, isn't he? I have been around a lot of quality guys, but he is the finest I have ever met. Don't look at me like that, because I know he is probably not ready for more than just friends."

"Hey, you are really wise. All the girls love Austin, but he is complicated. He really has never fallen for anyone. Not that you're not, but she will have to be something special. You give him space and time, and, who knows? We best be getting some sleep. Tomorrow is the first day of cheerleading! Good night, Anna. I am glad I have you for a roomie. I was not sure who I might have. You will do until I find a better one!"

Beth Ann giggled, and Anna threw a small pillow at her and they both laughed.

"You are okay too. Good night."

First Day of Football

Fred had been a favorite target as an offensive end for Austin in high school, and both looked forward to playing together. They were part of the team and were dressed out and on the field by seven to take advantage of the cooler temperature for the first practice.

The Arkansas Razorbacks played their games in 1940 in Razorback Stadium, which was constructed in 1938. It did not have lights at first, and all the games had to be day games.

At the first practice, Coach Fred Thomsen had everyone run for time in the 100-yard dash. Austin and a senior named George Talbert tied for the fastest on the team.

They lined up on the goal line and three of them threw the ball to see who could throw it the farthest. Austin threw the ball from the goal line to the 20-yard line. It was a throw of 80 yards in the air. George could only manage a 65-yard throw. The third could only manage 55 yards, and the coach and the team started to like what they saw.

Fred Tanner was just a couple of steps behind Austin and George in their race, and he was two inches taller and 20 pounds heavier than either. When the team moved to the contact drills, it was apparent both Fred and Austin were used to both, defense and offense. After a few minutes of drills, they began to line up in positions, and because Austin and Fred were freshmen, they were put on the second team.

The coach walked them through the few basic plays they ran, and was all smiles as he blew the whistle and sent them to the showers. He thought the team looked the best for the first practice of any team he had ever had. As Austin and Fred walked out of the gym locker room, the coach came up to Austin and shook his hand.

"So, you are Luke Johnson's son. I heard

about him and his brother, Levi, on the undefeated season team in 1909, and the next year when they lost only one game. He was a great player!"

"Thank you, sir!"

"Don't thank me yet. You have some high expectations to fulfill!"

"I am sure I do, but I can handle it."

The coach gazed at him for a moment, smiled, and said, "Just like your old man. He backed up his big talk though with a big walk. I am glad to have you, Austin. I want to meet your dad if he comes up. Okay?"

Austin smiled and said, "I would not have ever been allowed to go anywhere else!" They both laughed. "You will like my dad."

After several days of "two a days" the coach wanted to have a little scrimmage with the first team against the second team. In 1940, before the modern "platoon" system, most players played offense and defense. Austin was the quarterback on offense and linebacker on defense for the second team.

The kickoff was first team to the second team to show them how to do it. The ball was placed on the 40-yard line, and when it was kicked, Austin handled the ball. He took the ball and made a couple of steps as if he were going to the left. However, he reversed his field, and, with a good block from Fred, outran everyone to the end zone.

With all the interest in the new team, the stands had dozens of spectators. They went wild as they cheered on the freshmen, who never had scored much in the past.

The kicker for extra points was Austin who dropkicked the ball through the uprights placed on the goal line, and without an offensive play, the second team was ahead 70.

"Your turn, Talbert. Let's see what you can do!" taunted Austin.

"You were just lucky, Johnson. We are going to run you off the field!"

"You gotta catch me first."

"We can do that!"

The coach smiled as they lined up for the kickoff. He thought to himself, "This should be interesting."

Fred punted the ball instead of using the tee. The ball went over 55 yards in the air, and when it finally came down, George had just put it under his arm when he was hit so hard he almost lost consciousness. The ball came loose and Fred covered it. George groaned as he tried to clear his head, and Austin patted him on the chest as he pushed up off him.

"Get used to it, Talbert. It's going to be that way all day!"

After only about 60 minutes of action, while the coach stopped once in a while to point out a play or make a comment, the score was 280 for the second team. He blew his whistle and said, "That's it for today! Hit the showers!" He smiled a very broad smile.

Austin caught up with George Talbert who walked with a limp back to the locker room with his leather helmet in his hand. He patted him on the back and said, "It was not personal at all, George. It was just football. Are we still friends?"

"Of course we are. Anyone that can beat me around on a football field like you just did is my best friend! I am glad you are on my side. Come on, I'll buy you a Coke."

Austin, George, and Fred Tanner showered, dressed and went to The Little Pig Drive In. Austin and Fred went in Austin's car and George went in his 1937 Ford Rumble Seat Coupe.

It was a tossup, which was more fun; the convertible or the rumble seat. Both were very popular with the dating crowd, especially if one was to take his date to the Drive-in Movie or to the "submarine races."

The young men went inside and sat at a table with six chairs. They were ready to place their orders when a new, turquoise colored 1940 Dodge convertible drove up with a load of five University of Arkansas cheerleaders. Anna and Beth Ann were among the laughing group of girls, and came in with smiles.

As usual, Anna was the first to speak.

"I knew we would find you guys here after practice! Don't you ever get enough to eat?"

The guys laughed, and Austin said, "You know we always have room for a hamburger. Besides, we had our first scrimmage today, and we used up a lot of energy!"

"Yes, we know. It is all over campus the second team beat the first team! Oops, sorry George. I forgot you are on the first team," said Anna.

"No problem. We are all on the same team and that is all that matters. Your cousin is a great football player!"

"Yes, he is, and at least he is humble!" everyone laughed.

After they ate and visited for a while, George and Belinda, his fiancée, prepared to leave on their own. They were to get married when the school year was over. George was finishing a degree in accounting, and, he had been in the Army ROTC program at the University for the last four years. He and Belinda were to move to Washington D.C. after they were married. His dad was a Colonel in the Army and wanted his son to be on his staff. Colonel Talbert was a very influential person to know. George got up to leave, and shook Austin's hand.

"You know registration begins this week. So, the three of you meet me at the entrance to Old Main and I will help you get registered. I know all the teachers and can tell you the best ones to get."

"Why thank you, George," said Anna with a warm smile. "I am lost about where to go."

"It won't take long to find your way around. If football players can do it, you can do it too, Anna."

He smiled back, and Belinda took his hand quickly and said, "Come on, we better go!"

Austin stood beside Anna as the couple drove away. "Quite a little troublemaker, aren't we?"

"Okay, she may not ever be my best friend, but I am not interested at all in trading in my man Fred." She put her arm around him and smiled.

To have someone like the Senior, George Talbert, to help the group of Freshmen find all their classes, shortened the enrolling process. Everyone was ready for class to start the next day in only a few hours. Most everyone's classes were in the Old Main building, and it helped to find out where to go.

Anna was to major in education to be a physical education teacher back home in Little Rock. Austin and Fred both decided to major in Architecture like Austin's dad. He owned a major firm in Little Rock and was excited his son would someday take it over.

ROTC

Most of the young men had to sign up for Army ROTC. They received uniforms and immediately began to march all over campus to get used to the drills and cadence. Fred was shown by Austin how to keep his uniform creases razor sharp and his shoes were "spit shined" until they looked like patent leather. Both received a commendation in every personnel inspection.

The third week of school in ROTC was to be given to self-defense training. They had all dressed in regulation workout sweat suits, and Austin still managed to look neater than most of the other guys. A fatigue-uniformed enlisted man from the Army by the name of Sergeant Zeke Warner was brought in to train them in hand-to-hand combat. Austin watched the man a few times, as he threw the trainees around on the mat. After a while, he had bruised most of the young men. He looked toward Austin and smiled a sinister grin.

"How about you, lady? You want to try me?"

"What are the rules? I am not going to let you work me over like you have these others. Am I allowed to defend myself?"

The Army noncom smiled and said, "You can do anything you would like, but if I want to put you down, you will go down."

"Fair enough."

The two men circled one another warily. The sergeant was surprised at the grace and speed of this Freshman. He passed off every feint that he made with ease. All the college men yelled for Austin to pin him, and it started to irritate Zeke. He finally tried a leg whip to bring him down, but Austin stepped inside of his leg and grabbed him by the front of his shirt with one hand and flipped the man quickly over on his belly on the mat with the other. He put him in a choke grip before he could defend himself. The grip around his throat by Austin's forearm and the pressure of his hand on the back of his head caused him to start to lose consciousness.

"Okay! Okay! Release me! I must have slipped! Let's try it again and this time I won't be so nice!"

"Okay by me, sir. No broken bones or contusions will be the rules, but let's see moves a little more special than what you have shown us so far."

The man flushed a dark red and said, "Why you insolent.....!"

He came at Austin in a run, but Austin sidestepped him and knelt on one knee for leverage and almost threw him off the mat on his back. Before he could move Austin had his leg held straight and was starting to bend it backwards. The pain from the stretched ligaments in his knee caused the man to yell.

"Don't break it! I give up!"

Austin rolled over like a cat and pushed himself off the mat in a flip to land on his feet. He smiled at the man who held his knee and whined. He extended his hand and offered to help him up, but the man slapped his hand away and shouted, "Class dismissed!"

Captain Barry Bucholz, the officer in charge of the ROTC program, smiled to himself. He had never liked Zeke, and had watched the entire match from his office through a one-way glass. Nearly every semester Zeke hurt someone by being a bully, but this time it was his turn. As the men filed by his office, he opened his door and said, "Johnson, may I speak with you?"

"Yes, Sir! Recruit Austin Johnson at your service, Sir!" He stood rigidly at attention looking straight ahead.

"At ease, recruit."

Austin immediately snapped to parade rest with his hands behind his back, and his head up to look the officer in the eyes.

There was a little twinkle in his eyes as he could see here was a class act. He had already bested his best man in hand to hand, and he had seen him run all over a football field as the team won 380 on the first weekend of the season.

"Where did you learn the Washu? I have only seen the nobles in China use that form of hand to hand."

"You are right, sir. We have a main man or butler, or whatever, from China, which has been our caretaker for over 10 years. We have practiced every single day except Sunday since we were tots."

"I am impressed, Mr. Johnson. I will keep my eyes on you. You are an interesting young man."

"Thank you, sir. If I was out of line to Mr.

Warner I will apologize to him."

"Between you and me it won't hurt him to be knocked down a notch. He can be heavy handed sometimes. I liked it!"

Officer Bucholz shook hands with him and dismissed him. Austin snapped to attention, saluted, and said, "Thank you, sir!"

As Austin left his office, Bucholz smiled at his gung ho attitude. He thought to himself how much he reminded him of his own youthful fervor. He would keep his eyes on him. Men like Austin Johnson did not come along very often.

Austin became famous on campus after the incident in the self-defense class. Yet, even Anna remarked how unchanged he seemed to be. She had come to expect the unexpected with him. He was reticent and self-contained. He acted like nothing special had happened.

Football Season of 1940

The Arkansas Razorbacks were a very small team in 1940 compared to the other teams in the Southwestern Conference. Even with Austin at his best, the team went 46 with one win in the conference in the season.

With the war in Europe, young men from Arkansas went to the war in droves. The Razorbacks could not compete with the teams from Texas with much larger enrollments, which were hurt less from men enlisting. Austin and the rest of the team were glad when the season was over.

Fred and Anna continued to date and were alone more and more. Beth Ann told Anna she knew Austin in his own way liked her, but there was a part of him he continued to shield from her and the world. He was complicated as Anna had commented. He was fun, handsome, talented, courteous, but she did not believe they were connecting.

Austin went out with Beth Ann every weekend, and sometimes they hung out with Fred and Anna at the University Center. He never said they were going steady, but no one else ever asked her out. She was content to see Austin and be seen with him.

The weather turned colder in the fall, and most of the couples sat around the big fireplace in the University Center, or one of the dormitories, to talk and laugh.

Sometimes someone would play a guitar or even a ukulele. They sang some nights until the housemother turned the lights down. She gave them an extra hour on the weekends. She never smiled at any other young man except Austin as she stood by the door to lock it behind the men. He never failed to give her a quick hug and sometimes a peck on the cheek, which invariably made her smile.

The University of Arkansas shut down the second week of December in 1940 for the Christmas, or midyear, break. Austin took Beth Ann to the train station for her to go home to Alabama for the holiday.

"Austin," began Beth Ann, "thank you for being my friend this semester. I enjoyed the thought I was your girl. It made me feel like I am somebody special."

"Beth Ann, you are somebody special. I am only 19, and I do not have a clue where I am in life. I appreciate you not trying to put reins on me."

Beth Ann smiled and put her arms around him, and held him tight for a long moment. She looked up at him and quietly told him, "Austin, I am transferring to the University of Alabama in January. I will not be back even though it has been a very hard decision. My mother and I are able to communicate for the first time in our lives. She is not in good health and I will go back to Birmingham to watch over her while I go to school. I do not expect you to remember my name a year from now, but if you think of me, write me once in a while, and let me know what you are doing and where you are. Would you?"

"Yes, I will. Honestly, I don't know how often, but I will write at least occasionally, I promise."

"My mother is going to have a cow when she sees my short hair and new wardrobe! I thought rather than have her worry I would not tell her. I will just surprise her."

"Well, you look great, Beth Ann. I enjoyed taking you places."

They kissed for a long time, and she smiled at him and said, "I would get in trouble with Mother over that kiss, but it would be worth it!"

He watched her smile at him as she boarded the train. She found a seat so she could see him through the window. She blew one kiss at him, and then held her palm out against the window in goodbye until the train took her out of sight. Austin stood for a moment to gaze at the place where the train disappeared.

Austin drove home from school alone, and Fred and Anna traveled together in Fred's car. He followed the couple down Highway 64 through Clarksville, Russellville, Morrilton, Conway, North Little Rock, and finally into Little Rock. Austin was in a sober mood. He would miss Beth Ann for she understood he wanted his space and never seemed to question it. By the time they got to Little Rock and crossed the bridge over the Arkansas River, all of them were already excited and looked forward to John's home cooked meals.

When Austin, Fred, and Anna left for school it was Summer, and now the lack of leaves on the gray trees coupled with the amber grass created a mood of melancholy, which suddenly came over Austin when they turned off the highway and traveled up the drive.

They smiled, however, at all the Christmas decorations. There were lights wrapped around the trees in the yard, and there was a huge decorated tree shining through the windows as they approached the house. Suddenly the doors flew open and they heard James yell, "They're here!"

By the time the two cars stopped, they were mobbed by family. James opened Anna's door and got a big hug for doing so. John and Lydia came, bowed, patted them, and told them how much they had been missed. Fred kissed Anna quickly on the lips and said his goodbye for he knew everyone was watching. Austin and Anna's parents all came out to greet them, and they waved at Fred as he left.

"Hey look! Even Grandpa August and

Molly are here!" exclaimed Anna.

It was a joyous reunion. It had been several months since they had seen their grandparents, and all were excited.

August and Molly were in a new Lincoln. August still had lots of hair, but it was no longer jet black. However, he was still fit and handsome. Molly colored her hair, but she looked beautiful and robust for a woman of 70. After embraces all around, everyone went inside to sit by the fire. John and Lydia served hot chocolate and coffee for everyone. Plus, Lydia had already made the first fruitcake of the season in which she used rum for seasoning.

Luke kidded her by saying, "You know, Lydia, this is wonderful, but you need to use more rum!"

Everyone laughed and Lydia replied, "You know one cannot taste the rum after it is cooked. It only gives a pleasant aroma! I am not falling for that tease this year!"

After a huge meal and passing out gifts on Christmas Eve, everyone's conversations were on memories of Christmas past. The huge fireplace had stockings hung for every member of the families, including John and Lydia. Pine and cedar decorations were all over the room. The fresh scent reminded everyone it was Christmas.

On the mantle, was a wooden antique nativity scene, which had been lovingly hand, carved by Norman Howe, and painted by Bonnie, Maddie's parents, which had died a few years before within just a few weeks of one another. Norman died first from a heart attack, and Bonnie could not live without him. She died from a flu attack brought on by not eating. Maddie could not get her mother to carry on her life without him.

On a lighter note, Luke reminded Maddie of the Christmas back in Paris Levi proposed to Ellen, and he wanted to propose to her. She was not sure, and had even come home from college with another guy, Richard Allen, who now was an old family friend.

Maddie told the astonished Luke, "You know, when I saw the ring you bought, if you had went ahead and asked, I would have said yes."

"Now you tell me! Maddie, look how many years we could have been together if we both had not been so stubborn! I was not going to go ahead and ask when you had just told me you were not sure. I did not want to be turned down in front of everybody."

Maddie put her arms around him and looked into his eyes as she said, "Luke, if it is any consolation, I never one time thought I did not love you. The money turned my head for a while, but I did not want anyone, ever, except you."

"Good answer! Did you notice we are standing under the mistletoe? Come here, you!"

Luke held her off the ground for a moment

as he kissed her. As he let her back down, he smiled with tears in his eyes, "Seems like old times, huh?"

Winter 1941

By mid-January, after the Christmas and New Year Holidays, the schoolwork began to settle into a routine, and Austin began to study very intensely. He missed Beth Ann, but he had plenty of women to choose from if he needed to have an escort. His Architecture degree plan required several Math and Physics courses, as well as English. There was plenty to keep him busy and his mind from women.

"You know, Austin, I am worried you are not having any fun," said a serious Anna. They were sitting in a booth at the University Center with Fred.

"Would you quit trying to run my life?" he smiled.

"I am only trying to help. However, my dad is flying the plane up this afternoon to pick Fred and me up to fly to Birmingham to see Beth

Ann. Why don't you come with us? Her mother's funeral was just two days ago, and I am sure she could use the distraction too. We can stay at their big mansion. She called last night and she asked about you. I think she still likes you, and she needs you."

Austin heaved a big sigh and said, "Okay. I would like to see Beth Ann too. I really have not found anyone yet to take her place."

"I don't want to hear yet. I think you like her more than you know." When Anna smiled at him, he just shrugged his shoulders in answer and smiled.

"If I ever do have a wife I hope she does not nag like you!"

"If a woman doesn't nag, she doesn't love you. Don't you know that?"

Austin shook his head, looked at Fred, and said, "She's certifiable, you agree?"

"Don't get me in this. You are on your

own. The last time I confronted her, I wound up in the pool! Actually, my friend, we just care about you."

"I know you do, but I am fine. I promise. I will go pack a suit, and an extra pair of socks for the trip."

Anna smiled and rolled her eyes at his remark. However, she was glad she had convinced him to go with them. She believed it was best for Austin and Beth Ann. She knew both cared more than they showed to the world.

Levi and Ellen flew into the Fayetteville airport that afternoon around 2 p.m. They were in the Beechcraft twin-engine plane belonging to the family. It was used to travel back and forth to California for business mostly, but it had come in handy more than once to get people long distances in the shortest possible time. It had seats for eight not including the pilot and copilot.

All three were waiting at the airport with

their bags. Ellen and Levi went to the restroom, the plane was refueled, and they flew from Fayetteville to Birmingham on a cloudless day.

The group watched the terrain below. There was a surprising amount of green mixed in with the tan and brown of pastures and fields, which were being prepared for planting. Austin sat in the copilot's seat, and even took the controls until they prepared to land when Levi took over.

"Thanks, Uncle Levi. I have not been up for a while and I really have missed flying. At school, I have not had a chance to fly. It is a little hard without a plane, plus I am studying all the time."

"It has been great for me too. Your dad and I never got enough except when someone was shooting at us." Levi smiled.

As the plane landed, the black, Lincoln limousine belonging to the Davis family was there. As the plane rolled to a stop and the steps were put into position, the door was opened by Samuel, the black chauffeur, looking impeccable as always. Beth Ann got out quickly and ran across the tarmac. By the time she got to the foot of the steps, Anna was there to hug her tight as they both stood and cried.

"Look who else is on the plane!"

Austin was standing in the doorway smiling. He took the steps two at a time and swept Beth Ann into his arms and lifted her off the ground as he hugged her. He kissed her quickly on the lips, but both realized they were not alone. He put her back down, but kept his arm around her.

"Somebody had to come and keep Anna out of trouble!" All laughed as she made a face at him.

"It seems as if we have not seen one another for months, instead of a few weeks, so much has happened!" exclaimed a tearful Beth Ann. "I am so appreciative and glad you are here!"

Fred, Samuel, and Ellen's parents unloaded the luggage as Beth Ann walked between Anna and Austin arm in arm as they went on ahead to the limo. As the two girls got in, Austin helped load the final bags and sat beside Beth Ann. The big limousine held six comfortably, and, though everyone was somewhat subdued because of the circumstances, it was obvious the group was happy to be together again.

In the silence of the limousine, Anna spoke first, "Beth Ann," she began, and leaned across and put her hand over hers, "I know this is the most trite question in the world, but are you okay?"

"Yes. Yes, I am. Mother and I sat and talked for hours. She had been so consumed with making a lady out of me she forgot to make a daughter out of me. Those were her words.

We cried a lot because she knew she was very sick and was not going to see me finish college. She told me you were such a fresh breath of air compared to all the little old biddies she knew, and she wanted me to be more like you. I needed to be able to stand on my own. She even confessed she loved my short hair and brighter clothes!"

"Good! I was so worried she would blame me for messing you up!" The two young women giggled.

The Davis Estate was nearly as large as the Johnson's. The main house held the servants' quarters on one wing instead of behind the house as at Luke and Maddie's home. It did have a four-car garage, and Beth Ann said all the servants had stayed. In fact, she thought they were probably glad to be treated with respect. The atmosphere itself was lighter and laughter was heard in the house for the first time in years.

"Mother was not as mean as everyone believed. She was afraid to let her guard down and thought she needed to be firm to run everything. Mother had been such a part of my father's publishing business for years, that when he died after a long illness, the leadership transfer was seamless."

The group sat in the library around a warm fire in big, overstuffed leather chairs. The two pretty, light-skinned servants, Mattie and Hattie, came and went quietly as they served coffee and tea. Mattie had baked a cake and sweet rolls and everyone smiled and thanked the two women. Later, Mattie would tell Hattie how nice the visitors were. Most visitors treated them very indifferently, as if they were still slaves.

Austin had his arm around Beth Ann, and the two sat in a two-place love seat, and he looked at her and said quietly, "What now? Can you run the family business?"

"No, I won't have to. It is a corporation, and my dad's brother, Uncle Jim, has been the

CEO of it for the last few years and will take over for Mother. Daddy and Mother left 40 percent of the business to him. I have 52 percent, and the rest is owned by shareholders. It is doing well. I trust him, and even though I have had offers to sell, I do want to someday run it. I am majoring in Business Management already. Speaking of which, I have a surprise for you. Would you let me fly back with you? I have already reenrolled at the University of Arkansas and they even allowed me to continue to be Anna's roomie!"

Anna squealed and nearly jumped up and down at the thought of having her roommate back. Austin had a big smile as if he were glad too.

Levi and Ellen were invited to sleep in the Master Bedroom downstairs and there were shared rooms for Fred and Austin, and Anna and Beth Ann.

The next morning Beth Ann, as was her usual custom, got up early and almost tiptoed to the kitchen to not awaken anyone. She heard laughter coming from the kitchen. She pushed open the swinging kitchen door and Austin was visiting with Samuel, Hattie and Mattie.

"Oh, good morning! I hope we did not wake you. I was telling the girls how Anna threw Fred in the pool. We have a fresh pot of coffee going, want a cup?"

Hattie said, "I will get it for her. She likes a little cream in hers instead of black like you do, Mister Austin."

"I don't guess I ever thought you would be up early, Beth Ann. I was just making myself at home. I hope you don't mind. I used to get up early every morning and drink coffee with my dad before the day started."

"That's funny. I used to do the same thing when my dad was alive and I was young. It was our own private quiet time."

Austin smiled at her and thought Beth Ann

116

was no diva expecting breakfast in bed. He liked her more and more. Most of the girls he knew, which came from homes with money, were so spoiled he very seldom dated.

"Do you like cars? Let's go for a ride before everyone gets up."

"It is my one vice!" He smiled and said.

She shook her head and said, "Oh, really. One vice."

He smiled again and said, "Okay I guess I do like chocolate milk shakes. I am not perfect, am I?"

Beth Ann laughed, and though she was thinking he was pretty close to perfect, she said, "If that is the worse vices you have, we can make this friendship work!"

She put her arm through his as they walked out through the kitchen into the garage. There were several cars, including the limo under covers, but Austin saw a pair of huge headlights under one of them.

When he pulled the cover back, he exclaimed, "Wow! That is a Duesenberg! I have wanted one since I was a kid! Can I drive? I promise to be careful."

Beth Ann smiled at his antics around the dark red convertible.

"Men!" she said out loud. The "Doozie" had been her dad's favorite car to take her for a ride. It brought back so many pleasant memories of happier times.

"Sure. Let me help take off the cover. "

Even before the cover was off, Samuel came in and helped get the car ready to drive. It was a little cool for the top down, but he started it and let it warm up for them. Austin and Beth Ann were all smiles as the heater warmed their toes as Austin slowly backed it out of the garage.

"You be careful with my baby! I mean BOTH of them!"

"Trust me, Mr. Samuel, no one could appreciate an automobile like this one more than me. By the way, I have a pilot's license."

Samuel laughed and said, "You may be glad you do when you open it up a little on the open road!"

The Duesenberg was capable of 140 mph. This was an unheard of number for its time. It was the first automobile in America with hydraulic brakes, and a host of other ingenious ideas, such as dashboard-mounted lights to tell when to change oil (750 miles), a light for when to check the battery (1500 miles), and other inventions that cars only in the last few years had begun to emulate. The supercharged SJ model would run an eight second 0 to 60 with a top speed of 140. With a price tag of around 25,000 dollars, it was a very pricey toy for only the super-rich. Doctors and lawyers were making 3 to 5 thousand dollars a year. Gary Cooper, Clark Gable, Greta Garbo, and

James Cagney were examples of Duesenberg customers.

Austin had several pictures taken of him and Beth Ann in and around the car. He knew no one at school would believe he had driven such an icon of American conspicuous consumption.

Austin told himself he could never justify owning a Duesenberg. He was indeed a multimillionaire, but public scorn and opinion would just be too much for him to deal with at his age. For the moment, he had driven his dream car, which was enough. He did make a promise to himself to own one later.

On the plane back to Fayetteville, Beth Ann took a nap with her head on Austin's shoulder. Every time he looked at Anna, she smiled. He made a face at her, but he smiled too.

After Beth Ann moved back into the room with Anna, things got back to normal chaos at school. Everyone studied hard, but there were numerous good times of going on dates, walks hand in hand to class, basketball games, and as the weather warmed going into spring, the foursome would go on long drives into the Ozark Mountains.

One weekend they surprised Austin's grandparents, August and Molly, by driving up unannounced. Austin was concerned he was in love for the first time in his life and he needed advice.

While Molly, Anna, and Beth Ann prepared a big meal, Fred sat in a rocking chair on the porch. Austin and his grandfather went for a long walk out to the barn. Austin talked about his concerns while they restacked the hay and fed the livestock. After Austin opened up to him, his grandfather put his hand on his shoulder.

"Austin, you are my oldest grandchild. You have always been special to me for I can see a lot of your dad in you. You are mature well beyond your years, but let me say this. One of the reasons your dad was such a great wartime aviator is because he flew with such abandon. He took a risk for he knew the Germans were very meticulous about the way they flew. Your dad would sometimes fly upside down, as he attacked! It got to where when they saw his bright red, white, and blue wings they would break off and run for home. They called him the crazy American!"

Austin smiled at his grandfather for he had never heard that story. In fact, his dad never bragged about anything from the war.

"Look, my son, I am very conservative myself, but I can say this about Beth Ann and the woman she is, enjoy your time with her. I do think it may be a little early to start planning a wedding, especially with so much in front of you both. Graduate, and then make some plans for the future. Beth Ann loves you, and I promise you she is not going anywhere. She will truly be welcome in the Johnson family."

The talk with his grandfather eased his mind. After the trip back to school, Austin took Beth Ann for a Sunday afternoon ride to a park around Huntsville and Rogers in northern Arkansas. On the way back to the school, he stopped at a particularly spectacular view of the mountains and farms and houses far below. He put his arms around Beth Ann and said, "I love you. I have never told anyone else. I don't want anyone but you."

"You are something else, Austin. I love you too, and I do not ever want anyone but you." She rode back to the campus with her head on his shoulder and a smile on her face.

The rest of the semester included long talks between Austin and Beth Ann about goals and dreams, and what they wanted in a mate. It did not take too many times for both of them to realize they had something special.

Anna found Austin one day waiting for Beth Ann to come out of class. She put an arm around him and said, "You are in trouble, Austin. I know the signs, and you are in love with my roomie. However, it is extremely mutual. I cannot get her to talk about anything or anyone but you."

"Now, that is funny. My roomie said the same thing about me!"

"Ain't love grand? Well, gotta go, here comes your main squeeze."

"Such language! She is my ONLY squeeze." They smiled at one another as Beth Ann walked up to Austin and took his hand. After a quick kiss, they held hands as they walked across campus.

Summer of 1941

School was over in mid-May, and Austin drove Beth Ann to her home in Alabama. The servants were happy to see "Mister Austin" again. She had called to tell the staff to get the house ready.

When the few members of the Davis family came around to see what they could steal, they had had a confrontation with Samuel. For the family believed, since Mrs. Davis had passed, they were entitled to anything they wanted.

Beth Ann proved to have the mettle of her mother when it came to business. She made one phone call to the Chief of Police, who was a personal friend of her and her dad. He had seen Beth Ann on numerous occasions as she grew up, and treated her almost as a daughter.

He went to the man, who claimed to be a distant cousin, and collected a painting and some antiques, and explained in a very harsh tone, "Why didn't Samuel shoot you? I told him if anyone would not take no for an answer, to shoot 'em and I would rule it a justifiable homicide! Do I make myself clear?"

"Yes, sir." He hung his head in shame and he was very appreciative Beth Ann did not press charges.

"If money would do to me what I see you people do which have money, I would never want it! You never came around one time, when Mr. and Mrs. Davis were alive, to help Beth Ann care for them while they were sick. She put her college education on hold to come home and nurse her mother. Her mother dying in just a few days was in a way a good thing for Beth Ann. If I catch anyone on the property, I will arrest them! It is off limits until Beth Ann gets here in a few days. That's her home now!"

Samuel and the two women, Hattie and

Mattie, laughed at how quick everyone quit coming around when they related the story to Beth Ann and Austin. The visit by the Police Chief made them have a new understanding.

"How long are you staying, Mister Austin?"

"At least long enough to go for another drive in the Duesenberg!" He smiled at Beth Ann as she put her arm through his.

After a huge meal of Southern cooking at its finest with fried chicken, new potatoes, turnip greens, and apple pie, all served by Hattie and Mattie. Austin and Beth Ann asked all three of the staff to sit down at the table and eat if they wished, or at least have dessert and coffee with them. The little threesome seemed nervous as if they were concerned they were being let go. Austin and Beth Ann addressed their employment concern first by smiling at them.

Beth Ann spoke first to the little group. "I

wanted to thank you personally for your years of service, and want to assure you that you have a job as long as you want to stay. Austin is officially my fiancé, and we have talked at length about the things we would like to see changed. This is not the Old South. Hopefully we are a long way from slavery. I know what each of you makes in salary, and it is not enough to educate or raise a family. These three envelopes contain a check for each of you for one thousand dollars, and beginning this moment you will make a fair salary based on what you do. You are employees from now on, not servants."

The three black employees did not say a word for a long minute. They looked at Beth Ann and Austin as if they had not heard the conversation correctly.

"I just don't know what to say," began Samuel, the oldest at 45 years old. "We have not had families because we lived here. Although, I do have a couple of kids in town by a fine woman which I go see once or twice a week." He smiled, a little bashful at the disclosure.

"We knew, Samuel. We gave her a little money along on birthdays and holidays, and made her promise not to tell you! You have been here ten years and we wanted to keep you."

"And here I thought she was just good at managing her money!" laughed Samuel.

"What about you girls?" asked Austin.

"Hattie is 26 and I am 28, and we have had dates, but we could not quit working to get married. We give money to our mother who is working too. We have a little brother who is 20, and we are helping him get through his last year of college at Tuskegee. We want him to make a lawyer or a doctor. He has made excellent grades, and we believe he will not forget who helped get him there," confessed Mattie.

By then Austin was tearing up a little. He

thought about an entire family working for pocket change per day to make a difference in one family member's life.

"We would like to meet your family, including your mother and brother, girls, and your kids and wife to be, Samuel. Are you listening?" Austin looked straight at him, and Samuel smiled for he knew he planned for him to get married.

"Have the pastor of the little church you go to perform the ceremony in front of your friends and family. We want to be invited to the wedding, fair enough?"

"Yes sir, Mister Austin, and of course, you too, Miss Beth Ann!"

The staff was invited to continue living within the Davis house, but there was a new schedule and they were each only working 6 days a week, 8 hours a day. Hattie and Mattie alternated days off, and one worked early and one evening to continue coverage for meals and cleaning. Samuel had Wednesdays off completely. He was asked to leave a phone number or call in once or twice, if he could. Austin had his car if he and Beth Ann ever needed to go out, and the only time Samuel would ever need to work on his day off was something special. Compared to the schedule, which they had worked for years, the staff felt they were being treated more than fair. For the first time the staff was invited to use the swimming pool and outdoor grilling and party facilities if they were off duty and the facilities were not being used.

It did not take but a few days for the news to spread all over town concerning the changes at the Davis home. Jim Davis, Beth Ann's uncle, had been conspicuous because he had not already been by to see Beth Ann, and he called and wanted to see her at his office. She invited him to the house, because she did not want to go into town. He was there at two o'clock that afternoon.

Beth Ann went to the door when she heard the knock. She opened to her Uncle Jim, and he had a frown.

"Do you have to answer the door yourself these days? I heard you no longer have servants, only employees."

"If you mean Hattie and Mattie, I told them I would answer the door because it was probably you. Come in. Would you like a cup of tea or coffee?"

"No, I can't stay long. I needed to ask you what you are going to do about Davis Publishing."

"Why? Is something wrong? I have never received a profit and loss statement, and I asked the accountant to give me one."

He was a little brusque as he tried to hide his surprise and said, "Why, what are you trying to find?"

"Is there something I will find?" asked Beth Ann.

He flushed a little as he assured her, "No, nothing like that. I was afraid you were looking for something bad."

"Uncle Jim, I went to the bank and there is very little money in the accounts of the business or my personal account. Why is that? You told Mother we were doing well. However, you personally have several hundred thousand in your account."

"Oh, do you need some money, is that it?"

"The point is, I am supposed to already have money, and I don't. Against the advice of my lawyer, I am giving you 24 hours to do what you need to do to make everything right before the auditors come in. My dad and mother trusted you. Are we in agreement?"

"Yes, Beth Ann. Thank you." He treated her with respect for the first time in her life as he shook her hand and quickly left. Watching him drive away from the porch, Beth Ann smiled to herself. She was finally not intimidated by her uncle.

The audit revealed suspected wrongdoing, but several hundred thousand dollars appeared in Beth Ann's bank account and she declined to prosecute. She and Austin sat and talked about options.

"Some friends of my uncle have expressed an interest in buying the company. What do you think?"

"For you to run it, you would have to put your college on hold. Do you think you could trust your uncle now? If so, I think you should require consistency in profit and loss statements, and reports to find any irregularities before they happen. I know I am selfish, but I want you to come back to school with me. You can sell later once you decide what you want."

Beth Ann smiled at him, put her arms around his waist, and said, "What if I decide I want you?"

"That is a distinct possibility. I cannot imagine my future without you in it, Beth Ann."

There was a meeting with Uncle Jim, Beth Ann's lawyer, and the accounting firm she had hired. Austin was present, and Jim quietly and privately asked Beth Ann, "You are a very rich young lady, Beth Ann. You could probably cash out for over a million dollars. Do you think there is a possibility this guy from Arkansas is after you for your money?"

Beth laughed at him. "Don't be a fool, Uncle Jim. Austin Johnson is a multimillionaire, and his family is worth over twenty million. No, his family might be asking am I after his money!"

Jim Davis was stunned. The thought of that much money made him start smiling at Austin, for surely once Beth Ann and he were married there would be a way to get some of it.

"Will you be okay for a few minutes? I

need to take Samuel and go into town." asked Austin the next morning.

"Sure. Hattie and Mattie are helping me change the furniture around."

With a kiss and a, "See you later," to Beth Ann, Austin and Samuel drove into Birmingham and went to a jewelry store Austin had seen while on a drive to downtown. He went in and asked to see engagement and wedding rings. Samuel smiled and promised to not tell anyone he had made a purchase.

After the evening meal, Austin and Beth Ann sat out by the pool under an umbrella. The scent of magnolias permeated the air so heavy it seemed to be the air itself.

"We really have not decided where we go from here, have we, Beth Ann?"

"I don't know. Do you have any thoughts?"

"Yeah, I do. Let me have your glass. I will go refresh our drinks. I don't know where everybody is."

Over her shoulder, he could see three sets of eyes peering around the curtains. He went inside and put more ice in their glasses, and poured the tea. He pulled a little black box from his pocket, put it on the tray, and winked at the threesome who was smiling at him.

"Here you go. Have I told you lately I love you? I probably haven't since this morning, but I do."

"I love you too."

Beth Ann took her glass of tea from the tray and looked at the small black box.

"What is that?"

"Well, I'll be. Open it for I am curious too."

She thought Austin had purchased the new earrings they had seen in the window at the jewelry store. She opened it to see a huge diamond engagement ring. She looked at Austin who had a smile but had tears in his eyes.

"Beth Ann Davis, will you marry me?"

Austin was still standing, but Beth Ann stood, grabbed him and hugged him and shouted, "Yes, yes, yes!" The motion almost put them backwards into the pool.

From the doorway came Samuel, Hattie, and Mattie. All were in tears but were clapping as they gathered around the couple. "Miss Beth Ann, we know you two are going to be happy together. I am so proud for you both!" exclaimed Samuel.

They gathered around Austin and Beth Ann. Hattie and Mattie had already baked a cake.

"How did you know I was going to say yes?"

"If you hadn't, I would have run off with him myself!" laughed Hattie.

Beth Ann embraced the girls and Samuel. "Thank you. You are all the family I have and I am glad you are here to share it with me."

Beth Ann pointed her finger at Austin and said, "You are a little scamp! I had no idea!"

"Well, Samuel and I went to town to buy some things for the lawn, and I thought to myself, I wonder if Beth Ann would like to get married?" Austin laughed, and Beth Ann just shook her head.

"I think we could get married right here, don't you? My dad and uncle can fly everyone into Birmingham. I just want my family around, not a bunch of strangers. Plus, if we have it here, our staff can attend. No one makes a better cake than Hattie and Mattie."

"What about your folks?"

"Pack a few clothes and we will drive over and spring the surprise on them. If we leave around 5 in the morning, we can eat supper in Little Rock."

"Y'all start making plans for a wedding!" Austin told the jubilant threesome.

At close to 5 o'clock in the afternoon the

next day, James, Payton, Anna, and Fred sat by the pool and visited about Beth Ann and Austin. Anna thought Austin would like to marry her roomie, but he was so secretive about everything to do with his life she told them they would have to read about it in the paper.

They continued to laugh as a car drove into the driveway, and came around the corner of the house to the garage, which was close to the pool.

They heard, "Beep, beep, beep!" It was Austin's signature "horn hello!"

Austin had just opened the door for Beth Ann when the group from the pool plus Austin and Anna's parents hurried up to them.

With a big grin like he had been up to something mischievous, Austin stood with his arm around Beth Ann and said, "Folks, if you have not met her, I would like to introduce you to my fiancée, Beth Ann Davis!"

Anna jumped up and down and hugged

Beth Ann, while Fred and James pumped August's hand as if they were trying to prime a well. Luke and Maddie hugged Beth Ann, and Maddie exclaimed, "Finally, I get a daughter-in-law! You are so welcome into this family!"

Levi and Ellen of course remembered meeting Beth Ann when they flew over to Birmingham for her mother's funeral. They still embraced, and told her how glad they were for both of them. As they walked into the house, Anna walked between Austin and Beth Ann with her arms around both of them.

"Who would ever have guessed this would happen the day we met, roomie? Certainly not your mother!"

They smiled at one another, and Beth Ann said, "Believe it or not, Mother picked Austin for the man she wanted me to marry, and she loved you as my friend. She told me she could pass and not worry about me, because you two would take

141

care of me. Truthfully, it may be why she did not fight too hard to stay alive."

Anna pulled her to her body hard and said, "We will."

After a meal of sandwiches and salads fixed by John and Lydia, who were also proud to see the way things turned out, the group sat and talked about which date to have the wedding. When told Austin and Beth Ann were considering having the wedding in Birmingham, Luke said, "Look, let us fly over and pick up the staff and whoever else wants to come, and have it here in Little Rock at The Country Club."

Austin and Beth Ann looked at one another and Beth Ann shrugged her shoulders and smiled, "Sure. Why not?"

It was already the first week of June and it was decided to have the wedding at 10 o'clock in the morning on June 29th, which was the last Saturday of the month, because Beth Ann wanted to be a June bride. Plus, having it early in the day would help get away from the heat.

Maddie, Ellen, and Anna took Beth Ann the next day to buy her a wedding dress. They tried on most of the dresses in Little Rock. With her mother gone, the Johnson women decided they wanted to buy the bride a dress.

James was to be the Best Man, and Fred and Anna were in the wedding, of course, with Anna as Maid of Honor. The wedding was to be at the Country Club with August Johnson doing the honors.

Austin had several talks with his mother and dad and told them he was thinking about transferring to the University of Alabama in Tuscaloosa.

"Oh, my prodigal son! Don't break your daddy's heart!" Luke did smile, however, and ask why.

"Here is my logic. We already live on the

143

southwestern side of Birmingham and we could commute from our home to school. We will hopefully be able to not have classes every day of the week, and not have to drive the 50 or 60 miles round trip to school but a maximum of three days a week. If not, another scenario is to rent an apartment closer to school and come home a couple times a week. Don't look so serious, you guys. Alabama even has a football team! I have already talked to the Alabama coaching legend, Frank Thomas, and he said he would be glad to have me. Last season they only lost to Tennessee and Mississippi State. This year they are hoping for a national ranking. With my help they might!" Luke grinned.

"You mean to tell me my son is going to play for another team? You would lift your hands against your brothers? What is this world coming to?"

Luke laughed, but he put his hands on his

shoulders and smiled at him. "Your plan to move and live in Alabama makes perfect sense to me, Austin. Beth Ann needs to keep her house and business going. She has a great staff to help her, and with you by her side I expect to hear great things from you two."

"You forgive your prodigal son then?"

"Yes, and so did the father in the Bible, but I know a little now how he felt." Everyone laughed at the remark.

A week before the wedding, Levi and Luke went over in their plane and picked up Mattie, Hattie and Samuel. The girls' mother and Samuel's new bride also came.

John and Lydia were disappointed at first to not be doing the cake, but after Austin put his arm around them and explained the staff from Birmingham wanted to have a part, they were appreciative of the extra help.

John told Austin how much he understood

longtime loyalty. He shook Austin's hand because he had already heard of the emancipation of the staff and their promotion from servants to staff. He bowed to Austin and said, "I am proud of you. I taught you well."

Austin put his arms around him and said, "Yes, you did, old friend. Yes, you did."

After a catered wedding at The Country Club with all the ornate trimmings of expensive decorations, Austin borrowed his dad's plane and flew Beth Ann to Richard Allen's estate in Palm Springs, California. For over a week, the newlyweds were taken to Hollywood and toured Los Angeles and the surrounding beaches. Through Richard's connections as a movie producer, they met several movie stars and celebrities. It was a "dream" honeymoon.

Austin and Beth Ann flew back to Little Rock for a few days, and then drove their car back to Birmingham. The staff was glad to see the new couple and clapped as Austin carried Beth Ann over the threshold into the house.

"I am so glad to be home."

"Anywhere you are is home, Beth Ann."

Austin began a routine of getting up early and working out and running to get ready for football. Beth Ann played tennis and went swimming with him, and at times jogged along with him for shorter distances. By the middle of August and the start of "two a days'" Austin was a lean, tan, muscular, six foot two and 205 pounds.

The Alabama football team was coming off a good 1940 season with only two losses; Tennessee and Mississippi State. It was Alabama's third loss in a row to the University of Tennessee. The team went 72 overall and 42 in the Southeastern Conference. Acquiring Austin Johnson to be used on defense as well as wide receiver completed the team as far as Frank Thomas was concerned.

The 1941 season was an interesting one. Alabama beat Tulane 19‑14 in spite of being outplayed in yardage. Special team play and Austin returning a punt for a touchdown was the key to victory. Their record was 9‑2 overall and 5‑2 in conference play. It was successful enough to be invited to play Texas A&M in the Cotton Bowl.

Texas A&M out gained the Tide 309 yards to 75. Alabama made one first down and A&M made 13. However, unbelievably, Texas A&M had 12 turnovers, including seven interceptions and five fumbles. Alabama scored on a punt return and an interception return. Texas A&M fumbled on their 21 and 24-yard line twice and Alabama scored on both possessions. The final score was an improbable Alabama 28 and A&M 21.

On their way home from church on the first Sunday in December, people were running around in the street and shouting, "The war has started! The Japs bombed Pearl Harbor!"

148

All evening and into the night people were sitting by their radios and listened to the results of the sneak attack. The next day President Roosevelt declared war on the Japanese. Austin called home to talk to his dad. He thought he needed a point of reality.

"What should I do, Dad? With war declared, should I enlist?"

James has already called too, but I think both of you need to stay in school for now. Like the First World War, good leaders, which both of you will make with a college education, will be in demand. This will be another long and bloody war, my sons. Trust me; you will have a chance to fight."

Austin called James and invited him to Birmingham for a few days after school was out in May 1942. James drove over in his 1936 Ford Convertible. Although Beth Ann set him up with a date or two with pretty girls she knew, he explained he and Payton were close to getting engaged. The only thing keeping it from happening was the war and school. He and Payton were just sophomores at the University of Arkansas, and neither was ready for marriage, even though they were going steady and had been together for over two years.

In addition to home dates in Legion Field in Birmingham and Denny Stadium on campus in Tuscaloosa, the Tide played one game each at Cramton Bowl in Montgomery and Ladd Stadium in Mobile during the 1942 season.

A safety on a fumbled kickoff and a 38-yard touchdown run by running back Tom Jenkins were enough for an 80 win over Tennessee. However, in a game that decided the SEC championship for 1942, Alabama blew a 100 fourth quarter lead against Georgia. Frank Sinkwich, who went on to win the Heisman Trophy for 1942, threw two touchdown passes in the fourth, followed by a fumble return for a TD which iced Georgia's 2110 victory.

With the United States mobilizing for World War II and millions of men joining the armed forces, Alabama's schedule for 1942 included two games against military all-star teams. 'Bama won 270 against Pensacola Naval Air Station, a team that included former Alabama end Ben McLeod as well as players formerly of Fordham, LSU and Nebraska, but lost to a Georgia PreFlight squad that boasted former All-Americans from Tennessee and Tulane as well as other players with college experience.

Alabama's first ever Orange Bowl was a wild affair against Boston College. Alabama trailed 140 at the end of the first quarter, scored 22 points in the second quarter to go into halftime up 2221. They dominated the second half to win the game 3721. [1]

Christmas of 1942 was spent in Little

Rock. With nice sized bonuses for the staff, Austin and Beth Ann closed up the house and traveled over from Birmingham. James and Anna came home from the university, and it was a joyous occasion.

Two days before Christmas, after another huge John and Lydia meal, everyone was sitting around the fire in the family room. James put a log on the fire, turned and looked at the room and his father.

"Things are in chaos in the world, Dad. I have a friend on Guadalcanal. You remember Benny, I haven't heard from him or about him. I hope he is okay."

"Are you feeling guilty about not already volunteering?"

"Maybe a little. I will at least finish the school year, but I may enlist in the Army Air Corps. I want to be a fighter pilot. I already have a pilot's license. I have been told I could go."

"What about you, Austin?" asked Luke.

"I hate to say it, but James is right. There is already talk Alabama is not going to field a football team for the 1943 season. I want to fly also. I have been watching the progress of the new P51 Mustang and I want to fly it. That is one sweet airplane."

"Okay, what about you, Anna?" asked Levi.

"I have been talking to the people about becoming a WASP and ferrying planes from the United States to Europe. They would not let me be a fighter pilot."

"I have to tell you, kids, it breaks my heart to think of you in harm's way, but Levi and I went too. So, I am not going to even try to talk you out of it. I just will be praying for you every moment of every day."

"What about me?" spoke up Beth Ann. "I may not be a combatant, but what I do is also important. My publishing company received a contract from the War Department to print materials for everything from posters and propaganda to training manuals."

Austin put his arm around her and said softly, "Everyone is going to be just as proud of you as if you were a combatant. The war will have to be a team effort to win on so many fronts against so many countries. This is definitely a World War!" He kissed her on the cheek and held her tight for a moment.

The little group was quiet for a moment, and Luke said, "Let us pray."

Back home in Alabama, Austin and Beth Ann began to produce propaganda and training manuals while continuing to attend school. Beth Ann was impressed with how articulate Austin could be. He did most of the writing and she had to do very little editing to send it to the printers. The Navy Handbook required numerous pictures, and Austin took most of them using a press camera given to him by his Uncle Levi. It was left over from the days when he was a reporter for the Arkansas Gazette. After seeing some of his work, he told Austin he would give him a job, and Austin actually entertained the idea of being a War correspondent, but he wanted to fly.

In July 1943, Austin and James applied for Army flight school. After a 60-day officer candidate boot camp in Alabama, they went home for 10 days. Austin went to Alabama and James stayed in Little Rock. Both were Lieutenant Junior Grade after having two to three years of college and graduating from OCS.

Austin and Beth Ann spent every moment together at their home in Alabama. James and Payton at home in Little Rock felt they wanted to wait about getting married. In late October, both men received orders to Lubbock, Texas, for flight training at the Lubbock Army Airfield.

Lubbock Flight Training

Lubbock, Texas, in 1943 had a population of approximately 30,000, which grew quickly during and after the war. The city had given 2,000 acres a few years before to build an Army Training facility, and in the years from 1938 to 1943, Lubbock had trained several thousand aviators.

The training field was deemed safer than most by being surrounded with miles of flat farmland and blessed with a usually sunny, though sometimes cold in the winter, weather most of the year. It receives on the average of less than 19 inches of rain per year.

Austin and James rode the train from Little Rock, Arkansas, to Lubbock, Texas, in early November. "Is this it?" grumbled James. "The only green I see around here is uniforms."

"Welcome to West Texas in the

wintertime," smiled the noncom there to pick them up upon hearing the remark. "Don't worry, you will grow to love it."

"Yeah, I am sure I will," frowned James. He and Austin loaded their duffel bags into the Jeep and turned their collars up to the wind.

The ride in the jeep with no heater, and the top letting in the air with no windows, was bone chilling and numbing. Luckily, the train ran close to the main gate. The driver stopped at the gate as Austin and James presented documents, which allowed them on the base. The driver was friendly and even helped unload their bags in front of the barracks. He showed them where to find bunks and linens, and where the chow hall was.

"Thanks, man. I guess we are all set. We owe you one."

"Sounds good to me. You can buy a round at Pinky's. Oh, Pinky's is a local bar where mostly local veterans and soldiers hang out when we are not in class."

They both smiled and Austin said, "Will do! But it has to be warm. I am numb from the cold!"

The driver smiled back and said, "Know what you mean. I am from Arizona. You never really get used to this place!"

They found the man's name was Thomas Scott, and everyone called him Scottie. He was as laid back as James and he was well liked and a lot of fun. It was worth a drink just to get to hang out with him. He was only five foot seven with black hair and blue eyes. The girls stood in line to dance with him.

Austin called home collect just to make sure Beth Ann was able to take care of business without him. They visited for only about 10 minutes, and Beth Ann said, "Austin, don't worry about me. You keep focused on what you are doing. I am fine. Samuel and the girls are taking good care of me and send their love."

"I know, but I miss you. I love you."

"I love you too. Say hello to James for me."

"I will. I will call at least once a week. Goodbye, my love."

The first Saturday night on the base Scottie came by the barracks and told Austin, "I see you and James checked out a Jeep. I am going on in to Pinky's with a couple of the guys, and do a little "trolling" before the crowd comes. I'll see you guys there." He smiled and winked and Austin just shook his head.

About an hour later, after they had stood in line to check out the Jeep, Austin and James took two more soldiers with them and drove into Lubbock. Austin commented on the rough red brick streets of downtown, and then they drove out to "the Strip."

The Lubbock city fathers did not allow the

purchase of liquor inside the city limits, and the bars and package stores were relegated to a stretch of the Andrews highway south of town nicknamed "the Strip." To Austin and James it was somewhat hypocritical in that the bars were usually full of locals.

As the Jeep with Austin and James pulled into the parking lot, they saw a crowd of people watching a fight with three locals and one hapless soldier in a bloody uniform. One burly cowboy was raising his arm back to hit the soldier held up by two more laughing, drunk cowboys when it was gripped in a painful vise that pushed him down to his knees.

The cowboy rubbed on his forearm, which bore the handprint of Austin's grip. He gazed up at Austin and said, "That's quite a grip you got there, soldier boy."

The obvious pain showed as he stood. His friends let go of the soldier, and James caught the

161

semiconscious young man in his arms.

"Why, it is Scottie!" he exclaimed.

Austin turned and glared at the big cowboy.

"He was trying to pick up my girl. He was already dancing his second dance with her."

"Sounds like he had already picked her up. She probably was tired of an asinine buffoon like you pawing and slobbering at her. She wanted a gentleman."

There were several mutterings and a few laughs from the crowd who were afraid of Dixon and his rough friends.

"I have heard about men like you, Dixon. You are a coward. You are too afraid to go fight for your country, but to feel like a man you beat up young soldiers. Well, that stops tonight."

"You know, soldier boy. What do you think you are going to do? There are three of us and only two of you," smirked Dixon.

"You know, you are right." Austin looked at a redheaded drunk cowboy who was urging on Dixon. Austin pointed a finger at him and said evenly, "What about you, carrot top? Why don't you help Dixon and these other low lifes out so the fight will be fair? After my brother and I kick your butts all over this parking lot, I don't want anyone to be able to say it wasn't a fair fight, okay?"

The cowboy's face turned red from Austin's disrespect, and he started to take a step toward the two brothers.

Dixon put out a hand and stopped him. "No, he's mine. I am gonna carve him like a turkey," he scowled. He pulled an 8-inch bladed hunting knife from a sheath on his belt. He held it out in front of him and approached Austin.

Austin smiled at him, and said, "Hey, Dixon, watch this!" In one quick move, Austin kicked the man's hand and caused the knife to fly into the air. As Dixon looked up in astonishment, he did not see Austin's kick coming hard enough to almost crush his chest and send him backwards into the arms of his companions.

They held Dixon up as the knife came down into Austin's waiting hand. The two men's eyes opened wide as Austin jumped nimbly into the air and kicked both men in the face as they held on to Dixon. The Washu move caught both men by surprise as they fell back on the ground letting Dixon fall. Their noses were both broken and one had lost two front teeth. They lay on the ground groaning and looking at the blood dripping on the gravel parking lot.

"Okay, carrot top, your turn. It is just you and me!"

The man cursed and said, "No sir! I have seen enough. If you will let me go, I promise I will never pick a fight with a soldier again!"

The crowd laughed at the remark and carrot top's hasty departure.

Dixon was having trouble breathing from his broken sternum. He put his hand up and cringed as Austin stood over him and pulled him up by the front of his shirt with his left hand with the knife still in his right.

"Don't cut me! You win! I'm through!" He could barely talk, but his eyes were showing his fear.

"One last thing. I ever hear of you doing anything but buying a soldier a drink I will come for you and your friends. Next time I won't play. Do I make myself clear?"

Dixon was very polite as he wheezed, "Yes sir!"

"Now pick up your friends and go. I don't want to even see you for a long time!"

Dixon grimaced at the pain in his chest as he and his friends limped to their pickup while the crowd jeered and laughed.

Austin and James turned to look for

Scottie, and they discovered the pretty blonde cowgirl Dixon was trying to say was his girlfriend had Scottie's head cradled in her lap and was tenderly washing his mostly superficial wounds.

"Oh brother," laughed James as he rolled his eyes at the scene. Scottie opened his eyes, smiled, winked, and pulled the girl's hand back to his face and groaned a not very convincing sound. She went back to rubbing his forehead as he had his eyes closed and a smile on his face.

"Do you think he will survive the terrible beating he took from Dixon?" Austin asked with a big grin.

"He may not make it back to the base tonight, but, oh yeah, he is in fine hands!"

They both laughed and entered the bar, which erupted in a standing ovation. Even the locals had been afraid of Dixon and his cronies, but now it would take some time for their wounds to heal before they confronted anyone else.

Both brothers ordered their first beers and both agreed they could not understand why anyone would like that bitter taste. After forcing down two, the room began to spin, and they knew it was time to go. They drove back to the base where the officer at the gate saluted and said, "Thanks for taking care of a problem for our men. He had beat up so many guys we were told to go to Pinky's at our own risk. Glad to have you aboard!"

Austin returned the man's salute and he and James went to the barracks. They undressed down to uniform pants, undershirts, and socks. Both lay down to rest, and with everyone else in town on a Saturday night, they started talking to one another.

"Let's drive into town and go to church tomorrow," said Austin.

"I guess we probably need to after tonight," answered James with a wry smile.

The next day they went to the big First Baptist Church on Broadway close to Texas Tech. Both men enjoyed the service, and they were greeted warmly by the numerous service personnel and their families from the base.

"We are going to be okay, James. At least we have one another, and we know everyone at home is praying for us every day. Let's go find something to eat!"

Flight Training Begins

After two weeks of hanging around the base and watching the bulletin boards to see when they started their training, finally Austin and James were called into the base commander's office.

At a long table with stacks of papers in front of them, were three officers. The only one the two recognized was the base commander.

"I see on your application to flight school you both already know how to fly a little," the base commander spoke first.

Standing at attention, Austin spoke first, "Sir, we both have had our pilots' licenses since we were 16 years old. We learned to fly single and multiengine aircraft from being taught to fly the family's twin engine Beechcraft and the single engine Curtiss JN4. We both have logged over 1400 hours in different aircraft including the JN4 we were taught on, and I personally own a Piper Cub I am almost through restoring."

Astonished, the base commander laid his papers aside.

"Well, well, well, Mr. Austin Johnson, and Mr. James Johnson, that is interesting news indeed." The base commander looked at the other two officers and nodded as he smiled.

"Your country needs good pilots, but we also need men to train those good pilots. After your initial 7-month flight training, we will have two training billets here in Lubbock open if you would be interested. We don't need an answer this minute, but be thinking along those lines as you move through training.

Austin, I see here you are married. If you become a training officer, your wife could join you in on base housing. It might not be too bad in West Texas if you had your wife here. Besides, it might keep you out of trouble. I heard about the liaison work you two performed in neutralizing a local group of ruffians a couple of weeks ago. Unofficially, well done, but also let's remember why we are here, and keep the "making friends" to a minimum." He smiled, and when he did, the others followed suit. Austin and James snapped their heels together, saluted, and the base commander said, "Dismissed!"

The next morning was a clear, cold, West Texas day with little wind. In the cockpit of the AT6 Texan used for training, Austin listened to the flight instructor run through the preflight check as did James in his airplane. Both were going on their first orientation flights. Both had already walked around the planes checking the tires, free movement of the control surfaces, such as the rudder and ailerons.

When the instructors were satisfied with the physical condition of the exteriors, they started the engines and began to let them warm up to

171

operating temperature.

After the little JN4's which Austin and James had been flying, the AT6 Texan aircraft seemed to be a very advanced airplane. As the instructor opened the throttle, the plane rose from the runway very easily into the air.

They only flew over and around the base at first, and then climbed to an altitude of approximately 13000 feet. The instructors kept up a running conversation through the headsets as they pointed out local landmarks, neighboring towns, and navigation coordinates to familiarize the two with Lubbock and Lubbock County from the air.

After flying for about 30 minutes, Austin's flight instructor, Bill Burnett, asked Austin, "What do you think? Think you can learn to fly one of these?"

"Of course. Let me try it for a few minutes."

The instructor had seen several air cadets come through the training course, which could fly a little, but he was not prepared for a student who could fly as well, or maybe even better, than he could!

"I am impressed. Who taught you to fly?"

"My dad and uncle, who are twin brothers, were fighter pilots and flight instructors during World War I, and they have had James and me and our first cousin, Anna Lee, as copilots ever since we could sit up or walk. I had a solo flight before I was 12 years old, and my dad let James and me fly on every flight to and from all sorts of destinations. They have business interests in California, and even delivered the mail at one point, although the company sold out later."

"What happened to your cousin?"

"She is training to become a WASP and ferry bombers across to Europe. She's a pistol! If any woman can take care of herself, she can!"

Austin laughed. He then surprised Bill by doing a surprise barrel roll.

"This little trainer is really fun to fly!"

Bill grinned into his facemask, "Yes, it is! But you don't want the Old Man to know I let a new cadet do a barrel roll on his first flight!"

"I sure won't tell him, but it felt so willing I was never uncomfortable at any time, were you?"

"Nope, not a bit. I knew I could trust your flying. Let's head for home. It's a tradition the cadet buys the trainer the first round after their orientation flight."

"You're lying. Though I will have to remember that line when I train my own cadets." Austin laughed out loud. "I will be glad to buy!" He put his hand on his instructor's shoulder as they walked outside.

The North American T6 Texan was known as the "pilot maker" because of its important role in preparing pilots for combat. Derived from the 1935 North American NA16 prototype, a cantilever, low wing monoplane, the Texan filled the need for a basic combat trainer during World War II and beyond.

North American's rapid production of the T6 Texan coincided with the wartime expansion of the United States air war commitment. As of 1940, the required flight hours for combat pilots to earn their wings had been cut to only 200 during a much-shortened training period of seven months. Of those hours, 75 were logged in the AT6.

It had a maximum speed of 205 mph and a ceiling of 21,500 feet making it a forgiving, durable trainer.

Austin was even allowed to land the plane. It was a very soft landing and afterward Bill was complimented by the tower captain how well he landed. He looked at Austin as they carried their flight gear into the locker room, smiled, and winked.

Later that evening the foursome of Austin, James, Bill Burnett, and Dennis Duryea, Austin's trainer, were sitting in a nearly empty Pinky's Bar and Grill. They all got a laugh when Bill told the story how surprised the tower captain would have been to know it was Austin who had landed the plane, not him. Austin and James purchased a pitcher of draft beer apiece and the conversation finally took a more serious note.

Bill asked, "Have you and James thought any more about becoming flight instructors?"

"We have talked a little. How long have you been here?" asked Austin.

"I have been here 18 months. I love having my family here, but I am itching to leave and feeling a little guilty about not fighting alongside my students. I am one of the billets which, if you take the instructor position, will be replaced."

"How does your wife feel?" James asked.

"She's a good Army wife, and she knows how I feel. She and my son will move back to Russellville, Arkansas, to live in our home we left. You probably don't even know where that is."

"Sure we do. My dad and uncle grew up in Paris right up the road from Russellville. My grandfather is a Pentecostal preacher in Paris still today!"

"I thought you were from Alabama."

"I am from Little Rock, and met and married a pretty young thing named Beth Ann Davis from Birmingham, Alabama, which I met at the University of Arkansas. She has a business there and we moved to Birmingham to let her run it after her folks passed away. I transferred to the University of Alabama for two years before I joined the Army."

"Are you the same notorious Austin Johnson which played football for the University of Alabama just a couple of years ago?"

"Yep," smiled Austin.

"I happened to read about you returning that punt which won the game when you guys beat Tulane. Also, the bowl game against Texas A&M was on the radio. You were a standout there too! You had three interceptions!"

The only patrons in the bar were a couple of middle-aged people and a large table of Texas Tech students who had overheard the conversation about Austin. One of the students came over and spoke to Austin.

"I am not trying to intrude at all, Mister Johnson, but I don't guess you would want to play for Tech, would you?" said a smiling, slender, dark haired young man wearing glasses and a sport coat and tie. He had two giggling, blonde girlfriends beside him, which kept batting their eyes at the four young soldiers.

"Thank you for the compliment, but no, my football is put on hold until after my enlistment."

"Fair enough. We are glad to have you in Lubbock, and if you have a chance, the basketball team is starting to play conference games soon if you wanted to come and watch them play."

"You know, I would like that. Thank you for the invitation." He held out his hand and the young man shook his hand. The two girls and the rest of the table gathered around and shook hands, and both of the girls even hugged the soldiers. The men ate, finished their drinks, and left for the base smiling and waving at the students.

As Austin and James walked into the barracks, there was a note lying on Austin's bunk to call Anna at a phone number he did not recognize. He called the number and a female voice answered, "Women Air Force Service Pilots, to whom do you wish to speak?"

"This is Austin Johnson, and I am a family member of Anna Johnson. I missed her call and I am returning it. Is she around there close?"

"Yes she is. Hold on I can see her!" The girl held the phone and shouted, "Anna some guy is calling and says he is a family member!"

A breathless Anna picked up the phone and said excitedly into the phone as to who it could be, "Hello?"

"Hey troublemaker, are you still raising a ruckus? Where are you?"

"Austin! You won't believe this! I am in Sweetwater for WASP training just an hour away by air! How's James?"

"He's fine and here with me. We took our first orientation flights today. We are training in the AT6 and it is a neat little plane. I even did a barrel roll and secretly landed it on my first flight!"

"You didn't! They are so protective with us women it is boring. I have been meaning to call but I have only been here a couple of weeks and this is my first chance."

She got to visit for a few minutes with James and they all agreed the first time possible they were going to get together.

Both air-training facilities were shutting down for Thanksgiving weekend in two weeks and Anna had talked her dad into flying the family to Lubbock after picking her up. They would spend the weekend together in Lubbock.

Austin and James hung up the phone after visiting with Anna and both agreed it was going to be a long two weeks while they waited.

It snowed several inches in Lubbock the first of November, and for the first time, the Commander stopped all flying. The men played cards, drove a Jeep into town and smuggled a little booze back to the base. The base commander knew but with the war going on he pretended he did not.

On August 5, 1943, the Women's Flying

Training Detachment (WFTD) and the Women's Auxiliary Ferrying Squadron (WAFS) were combined to form the paramilitary WASP (Women Air Force Service Pilots) organization.

Twenty-five thousand women applied to join the Wasp, but only 1,830 were accepted and took the oath, and out of those only 1,074 women passed the training and joined, becoming the first women to fly American military aircraft.

After Austin and James left for Lubbock at the end of October 1943, Anna Lee joined the WASP. One of the requirements for all WASP was to have a pilot's license, and she had hers from the time she was 16 years old. Fred and she were engaged unofficially but he hurt his knee in training after joining the Army, and was transferring to Washington to accept an attaché position with Colonel Talbert, the father of George Talbert, his friend and teammate at the University of Arkansas.

The thought of being alone in Little Rock was a big reason she was ready to leave. Anna and Fred had talked before he left for the Army and he was encouraging her to join to get her to be able to possibly fly into Washington. She had arrived in Sweetwater, Texas, in late October, and was already flying training flights before she had the chance to call Austin and James.

Austin and James drove over to the Lubbock Municipal Airport on Wednesday afternoon before Thanksgiving Day to wait for the plane.

"Hey, there it is!" exclaimed James.

The stainless hulled Beechcraft gleamed in the late sunlight as it circled once and then settled onto the runway nice and easy.

"Must have been Dad flying," said Austin.

"Well, it probably wasn't Anna!" smiled James.

They were still had a smile as the plane

taxied to a stop and both looked at one another as Anna waved from the cockpit.

"I can't believe it!" laughed Luke.

The door opened and the steps extended and Austin was the first to the bottom of the steps. To his surprise, Beth Ann was the first one out the door and down the steps. She leaped the final two and Austin caught her in his arms and held her off the ground as he kissed her.

"What are you doing here? You did not say a word about coming!"

"The whole family cooked this up. We thought you guys might need a lift! We even have a surprise for James. Look!"

Payton was at the top of the steps, but James did not wait. He bounded up the steps and kissed her, and walked with his arm around her as they came down.

There were tears, embraces, and kisses everywhere as Luke, Maddie, Levi, and Ellen came down the steps. Finally, Anna came down after shutting down the cockpit.

"You know, Anna, you are getting better at landing. James and I were worried the Army would make you pay for all the crashed aircraft!" He held her close with tears in his eyes. She knew how much the three of them cared for one another.

"We had to have three Jeeps to get everyone picked up, and I got a guy to help us by driving one of the Jeeps. There he is now."

Everyone turned to see a uniformed soldier coming out of the terminal. No one said anything for a moment, and them Anna almost screamed.

"Fred!"

She ran across the pavement and into his arms as he whirled her around and kissed her. She furrowed her brow as she asked, "But how?"

"Ask Austin. He made a call to George Talbert, who asked his dad, the colonel, and officially, there happened to be a meeting come up in Lubbock. So, here I am!"

Anna turned to Austin, grabbed him and kissed him on the cheek. "I love you!" Everyone smiled.

"I will have to go by and give the base commander some papers from my dad for this to be a legitimate meeting." He smiled.

Later that evening, the little group sat in the lobby of the Lubbock Hotel and talked about the future. Fred had asked Anna to marry him and come back to Washington D.C. with him.

"Fred, you know the answer is yes, but I am still in training in Sweetwater, and I feel very strongly about serving in the WASP. I know your mother and dad are not here, but what if we got married this weekend, went back to work, and I will see if I can get stationed in D.C. after training. We will be deployed in over 120 different airfields, and several are around Washington. I am sure with your dad's help, okay, maybe Austin too,

186

I can be stationed with you." She smiled: for once a little bashful at the thought of spending the night with Fred.

Anna turned to her mother and Aunt Maddie and said, "Before you get too sad. Let me say this is not a spur of the moment thing. I promise as soon as the war is over, Fred and I will renew our vows and give you the pleasure of a church wedding. Fair enough?"

Anna's mother, Ellen, said with tears in her eyes, "The ceremony is not what marriage is all about. I would not mind at all for you two to have this weekend together. I know firsthand the uncertainty of war."

The day after Thanksgiving Day, Fred and Anna were married in front of Reverend Rogers of a little Pentecostal church in Lubbock. Both were in uniform as were Austin, his best man, and James as a male attendant. Beth Ann was Maid of Honor and carried the flowers for her while

Payton was bridesmaid.

Back at the hotel, Anna and Fred received an upgrade to the bridal suite complete with a bottle of champagne, which never was opened. It was cold outside on Saturday and it was about noon before the newlyweds made their appearance in the dining room. Both were embarrassed from the applause of everyone, which included even the patrons at the hotel when Austin stood and applauded.

Austin and James shook hands with Fred and embraced Anna.

"To think it all started with a dip in the pool!" smiled Austin at Anna.

Fred's return plane did not leave until Monday morning, but Anna had to be back before 10 p.m. Sunday night.

"It is just like being in college all over again," grumbled Anna. "Except here the house mother is a gripy old man." Then she giggled as she told the story of Austin flirting with the housemother at the University of Arkansas.

Anna and Fred were both trying to be brave for the other, but as soon as Anna was on the plane and airborne, she cried.

James and Payton decided to get married over the Christmas break and she would move to Lubbock to be near Austin and Beth Ann. The base commander was excited to have Austin and James commit to a year as training instructors after they received their wings the next June.

Austin and James both got a ten day leave for Christmas, and Luke flew the plane up to take everyone back to Little Rock for the wedding of Payton and James. Grandpa August agreed to perform the ceremony, and Austin was best man. Mallory, Payton's twin sister, was the Maid of Honor, which meant Austin was to be her escort.

"Well hello, Austin." Mallory came up alongside and casually put her hand on Austin's back. Austin turned and one of the first things he noticed was the big diamond engagement ring on her left hand. He was relieved a little because he believed things would not get out of hand, if she were already engaged. He wanted nothing to come between him and Beth Ann.

"Well, hello yourself, Miss Mallory." He smiled at her and said, "Who is the lucky guy?"

"Benny Winston has had a crush on me since we were in grade school. He was wounded on Iwo Jima. He was not able to do the physical work, and they sent him home. He begged me until I gave in! There were not any other rich guys around." She giggled, and just for a moment, he remembered how beautiful she was. He felt a familiar arm snake through his and Beth Ann's silky voice.

"Why, this must be Mallory, Payton's little sister. My name is Beth Ann, Austin's wife, and I am glad to meet any of Austin's friends."

To the casual male observer, it was a conversation between two women who had just met. The tone of voice, the direct eye contact, her arm through Austin's, and her controlled smile, let Mallory know with whom she was dealing. Beth Ann Johnson was a woman with a lifetime of dealing with forward little girls like Mallory, and she could more than hold her own as the wife of the best-looking guy at the wedding.

As a woman, the fact was not lost on Mallory, and she cleared her throat and said, "I better go find Benny. He's probably nursing a drink somewhere." She kept looking at Beth Ann but was pointing over her shoulder and waving at something vague. She backed into a chair but recovered her balance. Her eyes did not leave Beth Ann's.

"It was really nice to meet you, Mallory," purred Beth Ann as Mallory backed away. She squeezed Austin's arm to reassure him she had the situation well under control.

"Oooo. I could see the claws come out. You were something else! I imagine she will barely walk down the aisle beside me now. I have to admit, I have never been as intimidated by any man as Mallory was by you just now!"

Austin saw Mallory later at the rehearsal but she would not make eye contact. When it came time to link arms to walk the aisle, she kept her body well away from his. Beth Ann's point was made with Mallory. The savagery of women was not lost on Austin, and he just smiled to himself for he was very proud of Beth Ann.

After Austin, Beth Ann, James, and Payton returned to Lubbock after Christmas, the girls worked on decorating their little homes. Base housing was basic with gas stove, refrigerator, and furniture including bed, chest of drawers, chair, couch and coffee table. The girls went shopping nearly every day to find prints for the walls, rugs, nicer dishes, and curtains for the windows. They repainted with different colors inside and out, and within a few days, they were settled into their own first homes.

"Every day I come home it is to a different home!" exclaimed Austin.

Are you saying you don't like it?"

"No, darling, I was just making a comment. I actually enjoy it because I know you and Payton have to be bored."

"I have been thinking I might ride the bus to Birmingham for a few days to check on things, if you will be alright."

Austin frowned and said, "I guess I have been expecting it. We don't have kids for you to look after like some of the other wives, and you have a lot of responsibility as the owner of a business, which they don't even comprehend. I will miss nights and morning coffee with you, but I do understand. When are you planning to leave?"

"No big rush I suppose. This is Friday. What if I leave Monday morning? The bus leaves at 0600. See, I am learning military time."

"I will get permission to go in at 7:30. I can't stand the thought of not seeing you off!"

"You big softie," Beth Ann smiled at him and looked him in the face. She put her arms around him and squeezed. She smiled again and said, "We do have three days. We better make the best of it!"

The windup alarm clock went off at 4:30 a.m. on Monday morning. After turning off the alarm, Austin put his arm over on Beth Ann's side of the bed, but it was empty. He noticed the light under the bathroom door, and when he opened the door, Beth Ann was fully dressed brushing her hair.

"Goodness. You must be in a hurry to leave."

"The anticipation left me a little restless, and I could not sleep. You have a few minutes if you want to take a nap."

"I can sleep while you are gone."

Beth Ann left Lubbock on the first of February, but came back in Austin's car just in time for her birthday on March 17th. The party was held on the base, and friends and other instructors with their wives attended. The base commander even put in an appearance and got to dance with the "Birthday Girl."

"Are we going to be able to keep Austin here, Commander, after he earns his wings? He wants to be fighting so bad."

"Beth Ann, I know how he feels, but he settled down a little after I had a talk with him. If Austin went to Europe right now, he would do well, no doubt in my mind, but what if he could train numerous pilots to be as good as he is? He and James can make a very significant contribution to the war effort doing just what they are doing. He takes his training of cadets very seriously, and he will be able to produce some of the best pilots around which we need desperately. Honestly, I would really miss him."

"Are we both being selfish to not want to see him go?" she asked seriously.

"Probably some," he smiled, "but what he is doing is vital to our winning the war." He smiled at her as the song ended, and then he bowed a little bow and escorted her back to their table.

As Austin and Beth Ann got up to dance Austin smiled and asked, "Was he trying to get you to run away with him?"

"He asked, but I said no!" She laughed a small squeal as Austin squeezed her to him, and both laughed as people looked at them.

Graduation

On June 1, 1944, Austin and James graduated from the flight-training program at the Lubbock Army Air Base, and received their wings. The family had flown up from Little Rock and the base commander enjoyed showing Luke and Levi around the base while the officer's wives took off with the wives to eat some place fancy and encourage the wives with woman talk.

The next day they began their first training classes. The base commander spoke to the instructors old and new before he called a meeting of cadets and introduced each instructor.

"Men, within a week, the Allied Forces led by General Eisenhower will invade Europe in the largest assault in the history of warfare. There are several million troops involved. The cadets you will be responsible for training will be going up against veteran German pilots with excellent planes and nothing to lose. We are told to give them only 200 hours of combat training and send them. I understand the burden that will put on you and them, but we will do our best to see we send capable pilots to the front. God bless America!"

The men were dismissed to get ready for the first day of training a new group.

Each instructor was responsible for two trainees at first, but pilots were needed so badly the number jumped to four cadets each. Flying time was shortened to one and a half hours a day for each of the cadets, which made for a long day sometimes for the instructors. Morale was not a problem, but fatigue sometimes could be.

The instructors stayed in shape as well as keeping their minds relaxed by grilling out steaks, hamburgers, chicken, and getting together as much as possible. However, sometimes on the weekends, Austin and Beth Ann, Payton and James would put the top down, and go for a drive through the surrounding countryside.

Lubbock, Texas, is built on a plateau and sits roughly at an altitude of 3202 feet above sea level. There are numerous small towns, lakes, and parks including Ransom Canyon, Roaring Springs, and Lake Sweetwater, which is only a three-hour drive. It has been a spot for tourists and locals to swim and picnic since before 1900.

The foursome enjoyed their time off but Austin and James wanted to be in Europe to help fight the war from the cockpit of a real fighter. It was the main topic of conversation.

It became apparent by October 1944, when the Allies captured the German town of Aachen, the war was being lost in Europe. There was a seemingly endless stream of German troops from the front, which had been surrounded and then surrendered. Hitler's general, Rommel, committed suicide after the fall of Greece. No one but Hitler believed the war could be won, and the

Germans fell back to behind the Seigfrid line and began the Battle of The Bulge.

The Battle of the Bulge (also known as the Ardennes Offensive and the Von Runstedt Offensive) was the last major German offensive launched at the end of the war through the densely forested Ardennes Mountains region of Wallonia in Belgium, hence its French name (Bataille des Ardennes), and France and Luxembourg on the Western Front.

The Wehrnacht's code name for the offensive was Unternehmen Wacht am Rhine ("Operation Watch on the Rhine"), after the German Patriotic hymn Die Wacht am Rhein. This German offensive was officially named the ArdennesAlsace campaign by the U.S. Army, but it is known to the English-speaking general public simply as the Battle of the Bulge. The "bulge" being the initial incursion of the Germans put into the Allies line of advance, as seen in maps presented in contemporary newspapers.

The German offensive was supported by several subordinate operations known as Unternehem Bodenplatte, Greif, and Wahrung. Germany's goal was to split the British and American Allied line in half, capturing Antwerp, Belgium, and then proceed to encircle and destroy four Allied armies forcing the Western Allies to negotiate a peace treaty in the Axis' Powers' favor. Once accomplished, Hitler could return his attention and the bulk of his forces to the Soviet Armies in the East.

The offensive was planned with the utmost secrecy, minimizing radio traffic and moving troops and equipment under cover of darkness. Although ULTRA suggested a possible attack, and the Third U.S. Army's intelligence predicted a major German offensive, the Allies were still caught by surprise, due to a combination of Allied overconfidence, preoccupation with their own offensive plans and poor aerial reconnaissance.

Near complete surprise against a weakly defended section of the Allied line was achieved during heavy overcast weather, which grounded the Allies' overwhelmingly superior Air Forces. Fierce resistance, particularly around the key town of Bastogne, and terrain favoring the defenders threw the German timetable behind schedule. Allied reinforcements, including General George Patton's Third Army, and improving weather conditions, which permitted air attacks on German forces and supply lines, sealed the failure of the offensive.

In the wake of the defeat, many experienced German units were left severely depleted of men and equipment as survivors retreated to the defenses of the Siegfried Line.

For the Americans, with about 500,000 to 840,000 men committed, and some 70,000 to 89,000 casualties, including 19,000 killed, the

Battle of the Bulge was the largest and bloodiest battle Americans fought in World War II.

The best part of hearing about the offensive battle to Austin and James was a significant number of the pilots trained by them were instrumental in destroying or neutralizing the Luftwaffe for the rest of the war.

Austin, however, had become even more reserved and unto himself. Beth Ann knew it was because he felt his time was being wasted. His one-year commitment was up and he was to go before his base commander the next day.

"You want to go for a ride? I need to get out of Lubbock for a while. Pack a lunch and we will go to Ransom Canyon and eat."

Beth Ann put her arms around him and said quietly, "Austin, thank you for sticking this instructor thing out so that we could be together just you and me." She breathed a deep sigh and continued, "Have you thought about where you want to go? I want you to be fulfilled. I will go home to Alabama and keep myself busy until you come home."

"You are something else, Beth Ann. Your mother would be proud of you."

They spread a blanket on the rim of the canyon and she lay in his arms as they watched the last rays of the West Texas sunset turn the skies from blue to scarlet to indigo to darkness.

The next morning he knocked on the base commander's door and the attaché let him know he was there.

"Come in, Austin."

Austin stood at attention and the commander's face softened, for he had grown to have a lot of affection for this young man, but he also knew that it was time to let him go.

The war was almost over and he had done a job like no one else ever had.

"At ease. Have a seat," and he waved to a

stuffed chair to one side of the room.

The base commander sat down in an adjacent chair, and they both listened to an AT6 leave the runway and claw for altitude. He turned to him after a moment and quietly asked, "Where do you want to go?"

TForce In Germany

The Supreme Headquarters Allied Expeditionary Force (SHAEF) under General Eisenhower issued a directive to create TForce soon after the Normandy Landings. TForces were ordered to "identify, secure, guard, and exploit valuable and special information, including documents, equipment and persons of value to the Allied armies." TForce units were attached to the three-army groups on the western front; the 6th United States Army Group, 21st Army Group, and 12th Army Group. The targets of the TForce were selected and recommended by the Combined Intelligence Objectives Subcommittee (CIOS). TForce units were lightly armed but highly mobile.[1]

In post war Germany, TForce was tasked with carrying out abductions of German scientists and businessmen. One of the objectives of these abductions was to recover Nazi military secrets. In addition to this, the abductions of the scientists enabled Britain and the United States to use their knowledge to build back up the British and American economy after the war, and also prevented the Soviet Union from obtaining their knowledge.

For example, Courtauld's received the latest information on manmade fibers, Dorman Long benefited from information and equipment originating from the Hermann Goering Steel Works, and even the British coal industry had pit props sent to them from the Harz Mountains. On the military side much information was gathered, which could have been vital had the war in the Far East not ended so soon. There were wider political and economic implications, including the significance of the early liberation of Kiel, which prevented the Russians from adding SchleswigHolstein and the Jutland Peninsula.

Hans Gruber

Hans Gruber, former Nazi SS assassin, and now working for the Soviets, had been following the young American Army officer for over an hour. Hans had been alerted by a double agent on the inside of the occupying allied military about a secret document transfer, and was sitting in his car waiting for a courier to come out of the Army headquarters building.

After a while, a tall, fit looking, American Army officer emerged with a briefcase handcuffed to his left wrist. He looked side to side and got in a jeep parked at the curb.

Although he made sure he tailed him at a distance in his black 1934 Mercedes sedan, Hans followed him all over the city as the American ran a circuitous course to "shake" or lose someone if he was being followed. Finally, the man seemed to have convinced himself he was alone.

Hans sat in his car and watched the American park his jeep in front of the White Lily Pub and Bar. It was in a partially bombed out building, one of only a few with very little damage, not far from downtown Berlin. The young officer looked at his watch, got out of the Jeep, and started walking slowly among the burnt out buildings as if he were seeing the sites. He looked up and down shaking his head at the destruction, obviously in no hurry for his appointment.

"How trusting these young Americans are!" Hans thought to himself. He was confident this was going to be easy. He did not follow the young man, but was content to wait and let him come to him. He sat down outside the pub on the patio at a small table for two, and ordered a dark German beer as he watched him out of the corner of his eye.

The American, after a few minutes, took

another look at his watch and turned around to head back to the pub. Hans knew he needed to make his move before the officer met his appointment and gave away the briefcase.

Hans watched the entrance to the restroom. He knew most Americans wash their hands before they eat. The American looked around to satisfy himself his party had not arrived, and walked directly to the restroom, which was off the floor of the restaurant. It was down a small hall lit with only one bare electric light. The door opened outward, and once inside, the room had seen better days. It smelled of urine and filth from not having a regular cleaning.

It was dimly lit and Hans waited a moment to allow his eyes to adjust. At the other end of a row of urinals the young American was standing looking down. Hans looked and made sure the hallway was empty before entering. He shut the door behind him and started to reach for his Luger in a hidden shoulder holster under his suit coat.

"I've been waiting for you to make your move, Gerry. I have known since headquarters you were following me."

The slight drawl, thought Hans, placed the American as being from somewhere in the South in the United States. His hand froze on his pistol as he looked and realized the man had turned toward him. Hans was facing an Army issue Colt .45 in the hand of a young Army officer that showed no sign of fear or wavering.

"The war is over, you know. You lost."

"Not for me it isn't!" Hans' hand jerked on the butt of the Luger, and as it cleared the holster the American shot him twice, once in the chest. He staggered back against the stucco wall as his pistol fell clattering on the tile floor. His hand went to his chest and came away dripping blood, and he slid down the wall to a sitting position leaving a trail of crimson. As his eyes began to

212

dim in death, Hans could only cringe as Austin leaned over him and spoke to him quietly.

"That's where you're wrong, Gerry. It's over especially for you!"

Captain Austin Johnson of the 6th United States Army TForce hurriedly searched the man: found several passports, sets of papers, and a fat wallet with three thousand American dollars in hundred dollar bills. He took one passport for Switzerland and one for England. He also took out all but two one hundred dollar bills.

The door burst open and two Army MP's were pointing their own 45's at him as they stood in the doorway.

"Man, I am so glad you are here!" exclaimed Austin. "He drew a gun and made a grab for my briefcase. I had noticed him following me and so I came in here. I already had my pistol in my hand pretending to be going to the toilet when he came through the door. As he reached in his shoulder holster, I shot him."

The two men looked at one another and lowered their pistols. One of the men happened to recognize Austin as being from headquarters.

"Good job, Captain!"

"Listen, men, he obviously is a spy or assassin of some sort. I searched him and in his wallet he had a snapshot of him and a girl in front of a Nazi flag. One of the passports he was carrying is German and has his name as Hans Gruber. I am here to meet up with a British diplomat and deliver some important documents. Can you men take over from here?"

The men nodded.

Austin smiled at the two men, "I will be glad to say in my report the wallet was empty."

The two men looked at one another. They were used to finding people shot and having few facts to back up what happened. After the two hundred dollar gift, they were willing to swear they found Gruber already dead when they burst into the restroom, and they were not going to even mention the Army officer.

"Thanks men, I will see you on the base. I'll buy the first round!"

"Sure! Sure! You got a deal, captain! Get outta here!"

They both patted him on the back as he went by them out the door, down the hallway and out the back. By that time people were coming into the pub to see what had happened.

He jogged around to his jeep to find a pretty blonde woman in a British officer's uniform sitting in the front passenger's seat holding a large manila envelope and a small clutch purse. She smiled at him and said, "Captain Johnson, my name is Hannah Olsen, and I believe we need to have a sense of urgency about leaving this area!"

Austin grinned at the woman's use of the King's English as he vaulted over the door opening, turned on the ignition switch, hit the floor starter in the Jeep, and without spinning the tires, accelerated hard enough to push them both into their seats as they fled down the street and turned the first corner which came up after a few blocks.

Once they were a few more blocks away from the pub, Austin slowed the Jeep to just fast enough to have a conversation and still not draw any undue attention.

The woman said. "You can give me the briefcase now and I will take over from here."

Austin looked quickly at her and said, "I had instructions to meet a Dr. Barnhardt here and escort him to the British sector."

She smiled at him and said, "Don't you trust me?"

He had slowed the jeep to just more than a crawl to go around piles of bricks and lumber lying in the street. It was the shattered carcass of the once proud Third Reich.

He looked into her green eyes and said flatly, "No."

Flustered momentarily, she asked, "Why not? Don't I look trustworthy?"

"No offense, but actually I have not seen anything to make me trust you. A man I never saw before somehow knew I was coming, and tried to kill me in the restroom. I get to my Jeep and the most beautiful woman I have ever seen is sitting there. How did you know that was my jeep?"

"By the time I arrived, the jeep was the only military vehicle I saw."

"Where is your vehicle?"

"I was dropped off because I was told you would take me to where I wanted to go."

"Then how were you going to take over from here, to use your choice of words?"

Although her left hand still held the envelope, her right hand was in her lap as if to inch inside her small purse.

"Furthermore, Hannah Olsen, or whatever your name is, if you start to pull anything except a compact out of that purse, I am going to punch your lights out!"

She was startled for a moment by his sharp tone and quick transformation from a hillbilly soldier to a deadly foe. She looked at him for a moment, and quietly said, "I think you would, Captain Johnson."

"And another thing, how do you know my name?" He waited for an answer.

"Find an illuminated place where we can have some privacy, and I will show you my identification as a British officer. I am Royal Secret Service similar to you and my code name is Dr. Barnhardt. I was sent to meet you."

For the first time, Austin relaxed a little and even smiled, "Fair enough."

He thought, "Killing Gruber was one thing,

but I would hate to have to hurt a woman as beautiful as this one!"

Austin stopped the jeep under one of the very few working street lamps and checked her identification. He still held on to the briefcase, however. He would wait until they got to the British sector checkpoint and he could give the briefcase over to her with witnesses. Whatever was in the briefcase was important enough to have already cost one life, and he did not want the next one to be his.

The roughriding Jeep with Austin and Hannah Olsen slowed to a crawl as they headed for the British sector of Berlin. Austin could feel the hair on the back of his neck tingle as if there was a cross hair zeroed in on it. He looked right and left and watched the mirrors for any sign of movement as they crept along.

Suddenly, a black Mercedes Sedan similar to what Hans Gruber had been driving pulled across the street in an area of close quarters where the rubble only allowed one car at a time, blocking it completely.

Austin stopped the Jeep and as the window in the back of the car began to lower, he hit the bright lights, temporarily blinding the occupants of the car. He grabbed Hannah by the hand and half dragged her out as they jumped from the Jeep.

"PLINK, PLINK, PLINK!" the sound of bullets from a gun with a silencer hit the Jeep as they ran for cover to the first darkened building. Austin did not know how many there were; so he just kept low and kept pulling Hannah till for a brief moment they stopped in an adjacent building after entering on the ground floor and racing up several flights of stairs. They waited and listened. He could hear German and Russian being spoken and after some curses in German the men returned to the car and sped away as another military Jeep turned the corner.

Barely allowing themselves to breathe even though they were gasping for air, they listened to two men going over the jeep, who spoke in English quietly. In a few minutes, they could hear footsteps, and a voice said loudly but not yelling, "Captain Austin, is that you? Are you here?" It was the two MP's he had left at the pub.

As the men got closer, Austin said, "Don't shine your flashlights for they will know you found us. Is my Jeep okay?"

"Well, you got a few scars, but it is still drivable."

"Okay, go by it, turn off the lights and drive off. We will let you get about a block away, and then you turn at the first corner to the right and drive like Hades around the block and take up our rear! Got it? We will make a run for the checkpoint which is only a few more blocks, but I am depending on you two to keep them off us to let us get there!"

The two men were talking as if they had not found anything. They stopped at the Jeep, turned off the lights, and walked over and got in theirs and took off at a good clip but nothing to cause anyone to notice.

Austin and Hannah made it to the Jeep, vaulted over the door entrance into their seats, and Austin started the engine but did not turn on the lights till they were moving. Just as soon as he turned on the lights, he heard squealing tires behind him pulling from an alley. He floored the Jeep, and turned to the left, ran between two still standing concrete columns, killed the lights and pulled his 45.

"May I pull my pistol, Captain?" Hannah whispered.

"Yes, but aim it somewhere out there!" He smiled.

The black sedan flew by in a cloud of dust, and Austin grinned to see the MP's Jeep not far behind with the passenger pointing a pistol and shouting for them to stop.

With the sedan not worrying about Austin for the moment, they drove quickly until the lights of the British checkpoint appeared out of the fog. When he saw the British officer, Hannah, the guard held up his hand in the curious, to an American, open handed British salute as he passed her and Austin into the compound.

They pulled up in front of a well lit office building with several people in front, turned off the Jeep, and both took a deep breath. They got out of the Jeep, went up the few steps and into the outer office.

"Hey, Hannah!" cried one of the young enlisted men. "We heard some shots fired, did you happen to notice anything?"

Hannah smiled a little smile with a quick glance at Austin and said, "You know how it is. Could have been anything."

The briefcase was taken from Austin's wrist by a British Colonel, who smiled at the two of them but did not open the briefcase. He took it toward an inner office and over his shoulder said, "You are free to go!"

Hannah walked out the door with Austin as he went back to his Jeep. She paused and smiled at Austin as if there was something she wanted to say.

"I sleep here in the compound, and I suppose you are going back to the base."

"Actually, I have a room at a little hotel. As a member of TForce, I get a few perks. In fact, I have a few days off. I will write a letter or two and see if I have any mail. I may even drive around in the daylight a little."

"Wow, you are living the high life!" she smiled.

"Meet me at the Berlin Cafe tomorrow around 1100 hours, anywhere but the White Lily

Pub where we met! I will buy us lunch. The Berlin Cafe is where most of the officers from TForce hang out. No pressure, but I would like to get to know more about you."

"If you do, you might be disappointed. I am pretty much just a small city girl. But, I will be there."

The next day Austin was in uniform as he sat with a group of other officers at the Cafe. He heard one of them comment on what had just walked through the door. He turned and looked too, and just for a moment, he did not recognize Hannah. She was in street clothes, and she was even more beautiful than before.

Austin shrugged, "Oh, that's just my lunch date."

All the men were silent as he stood to meet her and escorted her over to a more private table than the one where he had been. The conversation waned as people stared, but started again as Austin frowned at them.

"Behave!" he mouthed behind her back as he escorted Hannah to their table.

Austin was amused and enjoyed the smiles and knowing winks and just shook his head.

"All men are pigs," he thought.

Even he conceded she looked hot. She was dressed in a form fitting black and white patterned dress with black high heels. She had on a white hat that was broad brimmed and turned down on one side to not only make her look gorgeous, but it lent an air of mystery to her. Every male in the place was staring.

Austin helped her with her fur wrap, and she smiled and purred, "Thank you, Captain Johnson."

Austin could have sworn he heard one of the men groan under his breath. The air was charged with excitement. Austin realized Hannah was used to just such reactions, but he still asked, "Had you rather go somewhere else?"

"Look, there is not a nicer place to eat in Berlin, and these guys are going to cry if we leave right now!" she giggled.

They both laughed as if it were an inside joke. She even went so far as to put her hand on his arm and lean over and whisper into his ear, "I know you are married, Austin, but we will give them something to talk about!" She laughed again, showing her pretty teeth and smile.

"You know, you are quite a wench! These guys are drooling. I hate to say this, but I would not be surprised that I could make a lot of money by auctioning off your phone number! Do women like this sort of attention?"

"What do you think? I rarely ever get to "walk the dog" as you Americans call it."

Austin laughed out loud at her remark, which caused all the men to turn and look at him, and he could see them mouthing obscenities in fun as he leaned over and whispered into Hannah's ear. "The phrase, Hannah, is 'putting on' the dog'!"

Hannah blushed slightly, but laughed as if at a very funny private joke. She put her hand over on Austin's forearm and put her head against his shoulder as she laughed at her obvious faux pas.

Several of the men looked at one another knowingly and winked, and one leaned back and put out his hands in a gesture as if to say, "Are you kidding me?"

No one but Austin and Hannah knew what had happened. After the meal the two rode around Berlin for a short time before he took her back to her base. He helped her from the jeep, and as he put out his hand, she kissed him quickly on the cheek. She smiled as he blushed.

With a few days of "down time" Austin drove around on the air base to the flight line to look at the row of P51 Mustangs. He got out and climbed up the ladder on one of them and looked into the open cockpit. He was dressed in uniform with his pilot's wings glistening.

"Hey, Captain Johnson, have you ever flown one of these?" It was Colonel "Big Red" Carmody from the base command.

He ran his hand over the cowl and said, "No, but I have always wanted to."

"Well, this is your lucky day. I can make it happen," said the man with enough gold braid on his hat to cause a solar flare. He was a full bird Colonel, and had been a squadron leader during the war. He confessed to Austin he was taking one up to just stay in practice, and he could fly wing man to help in case there were questions.

In a very few minutes, Austin had put on a helmet, jacket, parachute, and was climbing into the cockpit and getting a feel for what it must have been like.

He nearly shouted as the two planes lifted

off the runway. He managed to maintain enough of a straight face to fly alongside Colonel Carmody who was enjoying the flight almost as much.

"I flew high cover for bombers during the war as we bombed Berlin night and day. I never got tired of the feeling of diving through the clouds to engage the Germans in a dog fight. I have 12 confirmed kills of my own, plus a few more probables."

Austin smiled as he imagined what could have been. The two men chased one another through the clouds pretending to shoot at one another like kids with play guns tied to the handlebars of their bicycles.

"Hey, Johnson, you are a heck of a pilot! I would have loved to have had you as a real wing man!"

"Thanks, Colonel. It means a lot coming from you."

All too soon for Austin it was over. The men landed, put away the planes, and went to the ready room.

As they opened the door to the ready room, the base commander motioned for Austin to come to his office.

"We are not in trouble for joyriding in the Mustangs, are we?" Austin whispered aside to Colonel Carmody.

"No way, look at the brass in that room. It is something much bigger than that!"

Even the Colonel snapped to attention and saluted.

"At ease, men. I want to introduce you, Austin, to your next assignment. This is Doctor Richard Weiss. He and Doctor Einstein and Werner Von Braun collaborated on several projects for Hitler, and he would like to go to America and work for our side. It may sound simple but we need you and Doctor Barnhardt to accompany him. His English is not as good as his German. Hannah can speak fluent German, and she will be helpful on your journey.

"Okay, how do we get him out of Berlin? I am sure the Russians and the rogue SS troops are looking for him too."

"You are so right, Austin. The three of you will be shot on sight if you are caught. We are smuggling him out tonight along with both of you. There is a C47 loaded with a few farm tools ready to go from an old airfield beside the Rhine River. Can you fly it?"

"Sure."

"It will be dark in another hour. We can get you off the base, but after that you are on your own to get to that airfield. The plane will be ready to go."

Austin took Hannah and the doctor to another room to change clothes. One of Hannah's scarves over the Doctor's long hair and one of her work dresses started the transformation. She put heavy wool white socks and farm shoes on him, and with an old tattered work jacket from a janitor they had found he was ready.

Hannah told Austin to wait for a moment and then when she came out he could not believe it. She had on a male officer's uniform, and even a slight shadow mascara mustache.

"Maybe I am going crazy, Hannah, but you still look sexy!"

"You are weird, Austin. We have papers, if we can wing it a little, as two soldiers escorting a widow back to Britain. Pray we don't have to use them. I doubt if we will fool many people."

"I agree, most male soldiers are not as pretty as you."

She slapped his hand away and said seriously, "This won't be a picnic if we are discovered."

"I am not taking it lightly. How am I going

to explain to my wife if I get shot alongside you?"

"Maybe you better hope if you get shot they kill you, or your wife might!"

"That ain't funny!"

"It wasn't really meant to be. Okay, we gotta go."

The guard at the gate had been alerted to let the threesome pass because the little old lady was very sick and the two soldiers were taking her home off the base."

The guard at the gate was one of the MP's which Austin knew, and he just saluted as the threesome eased through the gate. They were driving one of the base command cars which was a Mercedes Sedan. The windows were darkened and Austin was pleased with the power of the engine.

The war was over, and there were command cars coming and going all the time. Going down the city streets the car just looked like it was looking for a place to eat or a place to have a drink. No one seemed interested in the car at all.

Downtown Berlin had been bombed without mercy, but as soon as they cleared the city there were a surprising number of homes back in use. Austin drove fairly fast but did not want to draw any attention. Soon, they saw the little industrial airport. The fuel trucks were pulling away from the plane as Austin came to a halt beside the runway.

"Hannah, I am going to walk across the runway and show the papers from the Colonel which state we are making a routine flight to southwestern Germany and Holland to deliver new farm equipment, and the little lady is very sick and needs to get to her home, which is just outside Amsterdam, our destination. As soon as you hear the engines start up, bring Dr. Weiss quickly and load him. As soon as we get him on the plane, no matter what happens, we don't stop. Okay? Make sure the Doctor knows what the plan is. He seems to be pretty spry and he may be able to pull this off."

Austin drove the car to the bottom of the on ramp steps and went up to the cockpit while Hannah, dressed as a soldier, helped the doctor carefully up the steps. They had just shut the door and an orderly was driving the car away when a black Mercedes car came careening around the guard shack.

Austin had already started to roll and he had the engines revved to the max. It did not take long for the plane to be moving fast enough the car could not keep up. A head and a luger appeared in one window.

"Get down and get behind something heavy duty. We are going to take some lead!" Austin shouted.

Just as the plane's wheels left the ground, the sound of gunfire erupted and there were bullets bouncing around inside the plane. Hannah had her body over the doctor and they were behind a stack of plow points on a pallet.

"Go! Go, baby, go!" She could hear Austin yelling.

The load had been packed light on purpose, and, as Austin pulled back on the wheel, they took a few leaves out of a tree top but they made it airborne!

As they circled for altitude, Austin was in constant communication with the base tower and received clearance to head southwestern for the English Channel. His code name was "Plow Point."

He was flying without lights trying to make it to the empty countryside before anyone knew. He had been alerted previously the Russians had two planes up looking for him. So, he could not fly at a high altitude and be seen on radar. He was flying very low and more afraid of hitting something than anything else.

Suddenly there were tracer bullets flying by the cockpit as a Russian Airacobra fired a warning salvo from behind him to try to force him to land. The fast moving Russian plane went up and over them. If they had indeed found him, Austin reasoned, he might as well climb enough to be able to maneuver. The idea of being a ground level, slow moving, unarmed target did not sound like fun.

The C47 with a light load climbed quickly to about 10,000 feet. He looked out the windscreen and could pick out the silhouette of the Russian fighter coming almost head on from a cloud bank. However, the Russian abruptly broke off and started a banking climb several hundred yards away. The Russian Airacobra was almost perpendicular when a P51 Mustang came roaring overhead with a burst from all 6 cannons. With a second burst, the Russian plane exploded.

Austin's headset crackled, "Hey there, Plow Point! This is your flying buddy, Ol' Big Red, and I will be an overhead escort to the coast. Have a nice day!"

"Thank you, sir! You're the best!" Austin exclaimed as he saw the fireball from the Russian plane drifting to earth and then explode. The plane with the trio aboard climbed even higher for the rest of the journey.

The plane landed in Amsterdam, and British TForce authorities came aboard and welcomed the group. They patted Doctor Weiss on the back and shook hands as Hannah translated to him he was safe. The look of relief and joy in the little old man's face brought tears to her eyes.

"I didn't know Brits ever cried."

"I think I have something in my eye," she returned, a little embarrassed that he had caught her.

"Come on. I will buy you a drink."

All they could find was a small, crowded bar not far from the base. No one was going to pay any attention to Hannah who was still dressed as a male soldier. They left the borrowed Jeep out front and went inside to order.

The Dutch had very good beer according to Hannah, and Austin agreed after he tasted the light colored brew.

"Are you going to be okay?"

"Of course. I am flying home to Britain tomorrow. I will be fine. I am taking an agent's position at British Intelligence. They will soon be shutting down the TForce."

"Sounds great. I'll know where to find you if I ever come to England."

"I am sure you will, Austin. You are going home and you will not even remember me a month from now."

"You and I both know that will not be the case."

Goodbye To Hannah

Hannah went to the airport to say goodbye to Austin and Doctor Weiss. They were flying back to Washington D.C. and Austin would ensure the doctor's safety as he traveled. From there he had a flight arranged to take him to Birmingham. It was the second week of December in 1945, and he wanted to be home before Christmas.

"Do you know which type of plane you are taking home?"

"The base commander told me we were returning a B24 back to the States. They are not taking any chances with us."

"Austin, I have to go, but you take care of yourself, okay? You are one of the good ones. As far as you and me; another place, another time." She smiled. She didn't kiss him on the lips, but she held him several long seconds before she kissed him on the cheek and walked away.

Austin picked up his duffel bag and suitcase and took the good doctor by the arm. As they walked toward the plane, he saw Hannah watching from a window. He smiled and waved at her and she blew him a kiss.

Once on the plane they had to wait a few minutes for the pilot and copilot. One of the men flying with them leaned over and in a joking tone said, "Believe it or not the pilot is a female! She probably wants to take one last look at the map." He laughed, but it died on his lips as he looked over Austin's shoulder to see the female pilot glaring at him. She had a short, blonde, stylish haircut, piercing blue eyes, and a frown.

"I suppose one of you guys think you could do a better job?"

Austin turned around when he heard her voice and stood up. "Dang right I can!"

The pilot opened her mouth in surprise before she started laughing.

"Of all the men in the world I know, you are the only one I would agree with! How are you doing, Cuz?" It was Anna Lee! She grabbed him and hugged him tight. "Austin, no one from home has heard from you in months. James will be home soon. He was a fighter pilot in the Pacific flying the Hellcat. He has made it back, but we didn't know if you were alive or dead."

"I am truly sorry for that, but TForce is such a secret, security conscious place that I was told to not contact even my wife until I got back to America. How is Beth Ann?"

"She has more Faith than any of us. She has never even considered the possibility you were not coming back.

I have a surprise waiting for you, Austin, when you get back to Washington. We land at 0600 their time, and I have been told a P51 Mustang is waiting for you to continue on to Birmingham. You should be home before dark. It is a perk for being a hero! Some Colonel Carmody put it together with a little help from General Talbert. I will visit with you later!"

She held him tight, kissed him on the cheek as she teared up, and said tenderly, "Let's go home!"

The cab slowed to turn in to the Davis Estate drive, but Austin stopped him and said, "I want to surprise them."

The driver smiled as Austin handed him a twenty dollar bill and said, "Merry Christmas!"

"Merry Christmas to you and yours, Sir!"

Austin picked up his bag and suitcase, patted the man on the back, and said, "Thank you." Beth Ann and the staff were finishing the evening meal in the dining room in the inner part of the house when the door bell rang.

"Who in the world?" said Beth Ann. "I am finished eating. I will get it."

The big, double glassed doors were cut to

see someone was there but it was so distorted all Beth Ann could see was a uniform. Curious and concerned, she grabbed open the door quickly.

Samuel and the girls heard her scream. By the time they got to the foyer, Austin and Beth Ann were both kissing and crying. Austin broke the kiss, and with Beth Ann's arms still around him, he reached and shook hands with Samuel and hugged the girls. Home!

After The War

Austin Johnson came back to Alabama from World War II in 1945 to the life he believed would be an idyllic storybook of love ever after.

Austin returned to the University of Alabama and received a degree in Architecture, and in the next few years, he and his best friend, Fred Tanner, built a thriving business as people built and rebuilt after the war. Homes and businesses were built at a frenetic pace as people went back to work with the GI Bill for service people, and easy money from banks and the government.

Fred Tanner, married to Austin's first cousin, Anna, shared the big estate house with Austin and Beth Ann, his wife. Neither couple had children, and Anna worked with Beth Ann at her publishing company. Their time together as part of the social scene in Little Rock was attending, or usually doing, a party or a cookout for themselves, the staff, or possibly friends. Life was good.

In late August of 1950, Austin stood in front of the bathroom mirror to shave while Beth Ann was downstairs in the kitchen. The windows were up to let in the cool, morning breeze. The door bell rang, and he dismissed it thinking it could be anyone. People were visiting often about business. If it was for him, he knew someone would let him know.

He took the last stroke, and rinsed the razor in the water in the sink. With a towel in his hand he walked over to the window. He noticed a dark blue, Buick convertible had pulled into the circular driveway from the opposite approach as most people, which meant the driver's side door was visible.

"I wonder what the mayor would want so early," thought Austin out loud. The mayor's blue Buick was the "talk of the town." He had only owned it a few weeks, and he alone drove it. His chauffeur was only allowed to drive the Estate Car which he used for public functions.

He heard a muffled cry and the unique sound of a pistol shot in the quiet morning air. He looked out the window and saw a man in a dark suit in a hat and gloves come running down the steps. He had a gun in his left hand, and he looked up to see Austin staring and snapped a shot at him as Austin dove for the floor. The man's smirk was forever etched in his memory. The man wore a black patch over his right eye, and he had a neatly trimmed goatee and mustache. The car had been left running and slung gravel as the man jumped in and sped toward the entrance to the driveway. He spun the tires on the pavement as he exited onto the street, and drove away.

Austin ran out the door to his bedroom from the bathroom. He looked over the railing and shouted, "NO!"

Austin descended the stairs in a run for he could see his wife lying in a pool of blood in the foyer. He reached Beth Ann and held her in his arms. She opened her eyes, and smiled a small smile.

"Do you love me, Austin?" she whispered.

He held her close as he looked into her eyes, "From now 'til forever, darling!" It was their pet term of endearment.

She smiled a small, wane smile, and closed her eyes. Austin tried to shake her awake, but with no response he held her to his chest and cried.

With a loud sob, Samuel, the butler, stood in the doorway and cried, "I tried to go and answer the door, Mister Austin, but Miss Beth wanted to do it herself. I am so sorry. I would gladly have taken the bullet!"

Austin raised his head and looked at Samuel. With a tear stained face and an expression set in stone, he whispered, "Go call the police chief and an ambulance. Tell them to hurry!"

Austin held his wife in his arms until the ambulance driver gently took her from him. He saw Beth Ann with a sheet over her face, and realized nothing would bring her back to him. The laughter and shared sunrises and sunsets were gone forever. The sadness and grief were almost more than he could bear. Austin laid his hand on her sheet covered forehead and whispered, "I will find him, Beth Ann, and I will kill him. I will show no mercy."

Austin stood beside the Chief of Police as he watched the crew load the body in the ambulance. He was still dressed in his blood stained undershirt and trousers. He was numb from the happening.

"Do you have anything, Chief Howard?"

"Yes, but you may not like it. We found the Mayor's car just a couple of miles from here. He had reported it was stolen this morning from

251

his front yard south of Birmingham. Also, this was handed to me. It was in the car."

The chief unfolded a handkerchief which contained a business card and a black eye patch. The business card had a hand written message. "To Austin Johnson, Heil Hitler!"

On the card was a blood red swastika in a red circle. Austin's anger burned within him for he knew there was only one place in the world anyone could connect him with an event and the Third Reich.

"Not much to go on, Austin. I'm sorry. He could be anyone, or anywhere, by now."

"Listen, Chief, we know this man did not drive here. We need to go to the airport in a hurry to see if he boarded a plane to Europe."

The chief sent a deputy and a detective in a hurry with sirens blaring to the airport. They were to check and see if anyone was leaving Birmingham with a final destination of Europe.

However, nothing of any interest showed on the passenger manifests. There were people on vacations and others on business. None were showing international connections. Whoever he was the assassin was very adept.

As a member of TForce at the end of the war, Austin had seen what they could do with only shreds of evidence. He took the handkerchief upstairs to his office. He did not allow anyone into the room except the chief, as he shut and locked the door. Carefully, he unfolded the handkerchief and laid aside the evidence. He picked up the card first with a pair of tweezers, and looked at it intently with a magnifying glass from his desk.

"The ink is India Ink, and from the backward slant on the writing, the man is left handed like the man who shot at me. Judging from the vellum paper and the impression left by the press, this card was printed on a hand press, and not a modern offset. I will need to go to Britain."

There was no emotion in his voice and, from the tone and the set of his jaw, the Chief thought to himself, "I would dearly hate to be in that man's shoes if Austin finds him."

Britain and Hannah

Three weeks after his wife's funeral, Austin flew commercial to Heathrow airport in London. He had left at night in the States, but it was about 10 a.m. when the Pan Am Constellation settled to the ground. Austin could not help but marvel at how smooth and fast air transportation was getting. He noticed they even had waitresses, called stewardesses, to bring the meals and wait on the passengers.

He had a cab take him to the Baglioni Hotel on Kensington Road. It was a five star hotel, and he knew the service would be the best quality.

He unpacked his bags, put everything away neatly, and went downstairs to the main desk. The smiling woman was helpful as she pointed him to a wall lined with phone booths. He had to change a few dollars into British coins to make the call.

He asked for the number to the British Intelligence Unit. He wrote the number on the inside of a matchbook cover from the hotel. When he asked to speak with Hannah Olsen, the man on the switchboard plugged into the office of the person in charge of international crime. The phone was answered by a female with a very smooth, familiar, but direct, voice.

"Hello, this is Hannah Olsen, Director. How may I help you?" The phone was silent on the other end of the line for a moment as Austin gathered himself.

"I need a lunch date and I was wondering, would you be free this morning?"

"Who is this? Do you have any idea of who I am? From your voice I can tell you are an American, but we do not carry on this way in the UK! What is your name, mister?"

"My name is Austin Johnson, and I need help. Please, Hannah. They killed my wife!"

"Oh my goodness, Austin, I am so sorry. Yes, we can meet. Where are you staying?"

"At the Baglioni, and they have a nice place to eat, would that be okay?"

Hannah thought to herself, "Of course, Austin would be at the finest hotel he could find." She set the time at 11:30, and Austin promised to go ahead and get the table. As Hannah hung up the phone she thought, "I should have worn something a little more stylish, but this will just have to do."

Smiling at herself for acting like a school girl, Hannah cleaned her desk and picked up her purse. She wondered would he have changed much as she opened the rear door to her corporate Bentley. The driver was used to driving Hannah places, but even his curiosity was piqued at the thought of his boss having a lunch date. She very seldom went out with anyone.

It was cloudy and drizzling as Austin sat at a window seat and waited for Hannah. He was grateful she would drop everything and meet him. He ordered a drink and watched the people; looking for anyone as if they could be a German assassin. He smiled to himself to think of the "cloak and dagger" assessment as if it were a movie. He abruptly had a thought which made his blood run cold, "This is for real! They shot my wife in my house, in my country, and I am here to make things right!"

Austin sat and relived the funeral and how he and the chief had checked every single spectator for a European look and accent. However, they knew everyone present and their families.

After the funeral, Austin had packed and made plans for the operations of the house and business. He gave his consent and Power of Attorney to Fred and Anna for them to be able to make decisions without his input. He had no idea how long he would be gone, and if he did not

258

come back the business and house would be theirs.

As he watched, a black Bentley came and stopped. The driver got out and opened the rear door for Hannah, extended his hand to help, and she got out gracefully from the Bentley.

"It will be a while, Charles, but wait for me. I may need to go somewhere else."

"Yes, mam." The driver was used to waiting for her and did not think it was an unusual request.

The doorman opened the hotel door, and she ascended the three steps to the foyer of the lobby. Hannah entered the quiet restaurant already looking for Austin.

"I believe your young man is at a table by the window, miss."

Curiously flattered by the remark, she smiled to see Austin as he stood and waved.

She walked up to him and offered her hand, but Austin embraced her for a quick moment which caused her to blush.

"Thanks for coming, Hannah. I didn't know where else to go but come here."

The tone of his voice was so flat and filled with determination it caught her off guard. He was very reserved as he pulled out a chair and seated her at the table. The waiter handed her a menu, and she ordered black tea and a salad.

Austin was already nursing a drink that looked as if it could be straight up Scotch. Hannah felt sorry for his loss, because the old Austin did not drink. She wondered to herself what else had changed.

Austin noticed Hannah looking at his drink. "Yeah, I know it is a little early to be drinking, but it keeps me settled a little. Don't worry. One is my limit."

With very few preliminaries, Austin described the scene of the shooting, and the shooter as best he could. He told Hannah about the left handed shot at him, and showed her the business card.

Hannah picked up the card, looked intently at both sides, and laid it back on the white tablecloth.

"Austin, listen to me. This is no doubt the work of Franz Gruber, the brother of the man you shot in the restroom back in Berlin right after the war. He has sworn vengeance on you and all members of the old T Force including me. The fact he was so brazen as to come to America, and had the resources that he could find you, should let you know what you are up against. He wanted you to come after him and you have."

"I figured all that out, and I am here to even it up. The war is over but I have read about the war trials and the German underground stating the war was not over for them. Fine by me. It is game on as far as I am concerned. Now, how do I find him?" His face was almost expressionless.

Hannah gazed at him soberly, and said quietly, "Austin, he is probably watching you at this very moment, but do not turn around. Have you a piece?"

"I have my .45 in a shoulder holster underneath my coat. It is by my side always."

"Good. Do you have any plans for the next few days? I have a small cottage not far from the ocean and isolated enough to be able to establish a perimeter. So, how would you like to spend the weekend with me?" She made a small, sideways grin at Austin. She was pleased to see the look of surprise in his eyes.

"Do you snore?" he smiled back, and Austin realized it was his first genuine smile since Beth Ann was killed.

She shook her head side to side to think he had said that, and smiled. "Okay, cowboy, my rules, my game, fair enough? I want to draw Gruber away from any crowds to protect innocent people from stray shots."

"Why does everyone here in Britain think people from the States are all cowboys? I do not even own a horse!"

"All the movies we have here from America are about cowboys. We think it is normal for you to be a cowboy. Pack a bag with a few clothes and a warm jacket. It gets cool here already mornings and evenings. I will pick you up out front a few minutes after we eat."

"Yes, mam!"

Both ate slowly and made small talk as they finished their meal. Austin was interested if she had a significant other, and the small moment of silence before she answered told Austin the question was not dear to her heart. She told him by way of explanation she just did not have time for personal relationships these days. They both stood. Austin held her chair, and for a moment he was close enough to smell her perfume and her hair.

He controlled himself with a deliberate smile, and gave her a handshake as they parted.

He walked with her to the foyer of the hotel, and as the doorman opened the door for her, he watched as the Bentley came. He waved at the driver, and then turned quickly for the elevator to his room. He was not surprised to see a shadow draw back from one of the columns, and knew he was being watched.

"No problem, friend. I want you as bad as you want me!" he said to himself.

Austin quickly packed a small suitcase, and changed into khaki pants, white shirt and a navy blue sport coat with no tie. He was wearing white boat shoes and black crew socks. He heeded Hannah's warning since it was late September and already cool, and put an overcoat over his arm.

Austin descended from his floor on the stairs instead of taking the elevator. He paused several times to see if he heard any footsteps behind him. He was disappointed he did not hear anything, for he was ready to finish the confrontation.

He walked outside of the hotel and put on his overcoat against the coolness of the early evening. He kept watch all around him for anyone paying any attention to him.

He heard the sound of a car horn. It was Hannah in a new MGTD. The little two seater convertible was dark green in color with a black top and a tan leather interior. He put his suitcase in the small back compartment and seated himself on the passenger's side of the right hand drive vehicle.

He looked around the very spartan interior, and thought to himself this was certainly a woman's car for someone with the idea of function over form. The seats were covered in leather; there was a radio, but no other luxuries. It was what he would have expected from the woman with such a job as the head of International Crime. She was all business all the time. He remembered how attractive she looked back in 1945 at the pub in Berlin. The thought of her and Berlin brought him back to the present.   Hannah looked at Austin sitting with his knees up under his chin and said, "Relax, that seat will slide back to give you more room."

After adjusting the seat, Austin smiled at her, "I was expecting the Bentley."

"I gave the driver a few days off. Besides, I wanted to drive my new car. I have had it just three days, and I have been going back and forth in the Bentley. I leave my personal car in the corporate garage. I had a TC, but when the new TD came out, I wanted one. This will be my first trip of over a few miles. I had to pick up a few groceries anyway."

Austin smiled and shook his head up and down to let her know he understood as she pulled away from the curb. The ride reminded him of his grandfather's Model T Ford. Still in all, he thought, it was sort of fun. The road became a wide, single lane as they left the city, and the serene pastures and well kept farms denied there was a war here once upon a time.

She drove quickly, but quite well. She used the brakes sparingly and down shifted for the turns. Idly, Austin figured the British Intelligence must give the agents driving instructions on how to drive fast.

Hannah's home was a small, nicely attended two story with a small garage attached. There was a small out building with flowers and shrubs neatly trimmed. Austin smiled to himself as he imagined Hannah working in her yard with sweat beading her forehead and coming through her top.

By now an interesting habit of Hannah's, she read his mind, and asked, "What? You cannot see me out tending my yard? It is a lovely way to unwind after chasing bad guys all day long."

The whitewashed cottage and buildings were on a bluff above an azure blue ocean and a tan colored beach. They were set back from the edge several hundred yards, and surrounded by a few trees and a six foot tall stone wall. The wall protected from the wind but also allowed no light from inside the house to be visible to the ocean. There was a long lane from the main road without any trees to be able to see someone approaching by vehicle.

The small beach was enclosed by high rocks, and a boat could only approach straight in from the ocean. The path from the ocean to the house was a single, Z shaped path of wooden steps cut into the cliff, and was over 30 feet tall. She was very isolated.

"Perfect!" thought Austin. He helped bring in the several bags of groceries and a couple bottles of wine.

The interior of the cottage had a polished stone floor covered partly with a nice Indian rug left over from one of Hannah's trips a few years before. The fireplace used coal for fuel, and, when lit, it was warm in the small house quickly. There were only candles at first, but Hannah pushed a button on the wall and lights came on.

When asked how she did the lights, Hannah lifted a corner of the rug, pulled up a small section of stone, and took Austin down a flight of stairs to the basement. She pulled an invisible latch and one wall divided and slid apart to reveal an oil burning generator and a modern shortwave radio.

"My contact to the outside world."

"Wow, I am impressed."

She opened a large cabinet which took up an entire wall, and it was filled with pistols, automatic rifles, throwing knives, and other armaments of all sorts. There was even a grenade launcher which Austin picked up to inspect.

Hannah smiled and with a shrug said, "In case we need to defend ourselves."

"Who were you expecting, the Russian Army?"

"Well, seriously, out here one would not be able to call in backup from town quickly. My plan would be to make a call and then hold them off until help arrived."

"Well, I think with all this it is a good plan. Did you bring anything to eat? I was so interested in seeing you I did not eat much at lunch."

"Come sit at the table, and let's visit while I make us something to eat."

Austin smiled warmly, "I used to do the same thing when I was at home. I am not a bad cook myself on every day dishes. Do you have any pinto beans and cornbread?"

Hannah giggled. "Sorry, my friend. We do

not eat beans and cornbread around here. I might try it some time, however, if you will cook."

"I can do it."

After the meal of panfried beef and potatoes, Austin picked up his plate and started for the sink.

"What are you doing?"

"Old habits die hard I guess. You sit there, and because you cooked I will clear the table."

Hannah crossed her arms and smiled.

"You are the first man I have ever seen that would even think to clear the table. Go ahead. I will let you."

Up until that moment, Hannah had never considered Austin anything but an acquaintance, but to herself she could imagine a fantasy scenario of the two of them in a long relationship, especially if he was willing to pick up after himself. The smile stayed on her face as she watched Austin. She was very impressed with how efficient he was, and his attention to detail made her begin to think he was a lot more than what she had ever imagined.

"You did this for your wife, did you not? I thought you had servants."

"We had employees, not servants. When just my wife and I fixed, we did our own cleanup. Usually that was me if she cooked."

The sudden solemn look on his face made her change the subject.

"Let me open some wine and we can move into the living area to visit."

Within just a few minutes, the kitchen was spotless once again with everything back in its place. Austin dried his hands on a cup towel, folded it neatly, and put it beside the sink. He sat in one of the two chairs placed at either end of a matching couch, and Hannah sat on the other. All the pieces of furniture were over stuffed, comfortable, and leather covered. Austin idly wondered if there were any "stories" the couch could tell. The thought brought a small grin as he looked at Hannah sitting with her legs folded under her like a little girl and a blanket across her lap.

"Do not even think it! The only other man who has ever been in this house besides you is Patrick Donovan, the old man from down the way who checks on my place when I am away. I tell him if I am going to be away for more than a couple of days. He only comes inside when I am here. I have never shown him the basement with the generator and the radio. He thinks I am a government employee and I just want my privacy. Actually, he is right."

"You frighten me, Hannah," he kidded her. "I know my thoughts might be obvious sometimes, but for you to be able to read my mind of even my most private thoughts makes me very nervous. I am not used to it. I am a very private person most times."

His obvious sincerity made her laugh, showing a pretty set of teeth and dimples.

"Austin, I know men better than you know women. Look at me. I have been hit on by almost every man I have ever met. I dress very prim and proper at work for men to take me serious. I am very good at what I do, and to be thought of as proficient means a lot to me."

"Fair enough, but I would be willing to bet there are lots of situations when you are under estimated. That could be a good thing at times, right?"

Hannah smiled a small smile as if to agree without having to say so.

"Now," began Austin. "How do you think Gruber found me in America? Do you have a mole?"

"About a year ago, a piece on the old TForce was written in the London newspaper which mentioned the American soldier from Birmingham, Alabama, who had smuggled out Doctor Weiss from under the noses of the Germans and the Russians. I was mentioned, but by description only. However, how many blondes did we have in the TForce? I was the only local blonde from several."

"Why haven't you picked him up or used a double O to take him out?"

"We have been close, but he is very good and very cautious. Plus, it has only been in the last six months he has shown any aggression. We thought the old SS was gone, but it seems in the new Cold War with the Americans, the Germans are only too glad to have the Russian KGB on their side. The same goes for the KGB. The SS are already trained assassins and have nothing to lose. It is a most deadly combination. That is why I have a proposition for you."

As Austin smiled a lascivious grin, Hannah

smiled and said, "Austin, any woman in the world would know you picked up on the word proposition. I did not have to read your mind!"

"Okay, my bad." They both laughed for a moment, but the laughter stopped as they looked at one another steadily. They both thought the term might be a possibility at some point in time.

"Austin, I might be able to get you a commission with British Intelligence since you were part of the TForce in the war to allow you some cover for what you want to do. Plus, we need help very badly. Britain lost lots of good men in the war."

Austin nodded grimly, "We all did."

Austin was quiet for a moment as he thought about Hannah's offer. He knew she was right and that he needed help to find Gruber. In the mean time he could help the Intelligence Agency in their cause against the KGB. However, he wanted to know more.

"What do I have to do? Will I have an extended training? I don't want to spend a year or two chasing shadows while Gruber is on the loose. Can you help me there?"

"Don't worry. We need you in the field as soon as possible. A few weeks of orientation to see where you would best serve, and we will need you to train on the new technology which is changing all the time. We have hand held radios, for example, which are so small they can be carried in the pocket."

"What about physical training?"

"You won't have any problem."

Training

After three long days of physical and mental tests, Austin was pronounced fit enough to continue training. Hannah was kept informed of his progress, and was impressed at the comments of his trainers. To a person, all considered Austin to be the finest example of a recruit they had seen in a long time.

On the firing range, Austin shot expert using the regulation Walther pistol. He bested the instructor in hand to hand training, and in the classroom proved to be very intelligent and articulate despite a slight Southern drawl.

Because he was only attached to the British Intelligence he was allowed to keep his suite at the hotel at his own expense. Hannah sent the Bentley for him every morning, and usually she took him home to his hotel after dinner in the evening in her car. It was not uncommon for them to meet other agents after work for a drink or two. Hannah seemed to be happy with having Austin for a friend to just talk and have a meal.

Austin was introduced to darts and found he had a certain knack for the game. He became very good in just a few weeks. By being able to stand he could watch the room. He felt he was less of a target than sitting still where a knife or a long shot could get to him.

The days passed quickly. One cold, late November evening he and Hannah were walking the few feet to the curb to wait for the car arm in arm. They paused in a dark doorway just outside the door of the "Little Pig Pub" waiting for the Bentley.

He had noticed a black sedan a little over a block away. It was not under a street light and without the headlights on it was hard to tell if there was anyone at the wheel. He had only glanced up and down the street, but the old feeling he picked up during the war when something was not right made him slide his hand under his overcoat and loosen his Beretta. He wished he still had his 45.

He put his arm around Hannah and started to tell of the car but she smiled up at him and said quietly, "Yes, I saw it too. I took out my compact but I held on to my pistol in case there is going to be trouble."

Austin pretended to laugh hard as if it were just a casual conversation while he monitored the street. The car rolled forward without any lights and Austin paused, looked at Hannah, and smiled grimly, "Don't get upset, but here it comes!"

Before she could protest, Austin put his back to the car coming up the street, pulled her to him and kissed her. He held the kiss mouth to mouth as he watched the car in the store window. Suddenly the car surged forward as the driver turned on the lights to mask himself and floored the accelerator. He released Hannah and pushed her to one side. He yanked his pistol and kneeled on one knee as the car was now about 50 yards away. He pointed the gun at the driver, but decided on the car instead.

The first two shots Austin shot out the lights, and he could see a pistol trying to get a bead on him as he moved closer. A shot from the car pinged off the brick where his head had been before; Austin fired another two quick rounds through the windshield. The man obviously was hit as he dropped his pistol and ducked back inside the car. The car swerved into the middle of the street, and Austin kept firing until the clip was empty.

The car was out of control. The sedan hit the curb on the concrete median and rolled over once and back upright onto its tires.

As Austin ran toward the car he put in a fresh clip. Not seeing or hearing any movement, he bent over from the back of the car to look through the rear window. He could see a head lying back on the seat. He cautiously approached the car from the driver's side and quickly glanced inside.

"He's dead, isn't he?" whispered a mildly shaken Hannah from beside him with her gun still drawn.

"I'm afraid so. A nine millimeter in the forehead does it every time." He smiled grimly at her as he continued.

"I hit him three times; once was in the throat, another in the chest, besides the round in the forehead."

"Here comes the Bentley along with nearly every police car in London!" exclaimed Hannah.

After a few minutes of showing credentials, the police took over the investigation. The shooter was not Gruber, but he was known to be a part of his team. Austin and Hannah had

David, the new Bentley driver, take them back to Austin's hotel to not have a long drive to her home so late at night. The straight faced driver smiled, and his sly smile quickly faded when Hannah glared at him and said, "What?"

She squeezed Austin's arm to let him know how amusing she thought the whole thing was. However, the actual thought of a night in a hotel alone with Austin made her face turn red. She turned away to not let Austin see. She did not want to face any kidding.

At the front desk of the hotel, the man handed the key to Austin with typical British aplomb as if he were just another customer. One would never guess the customer had just shot a man outside the hotel. Hannah had a small suitcase with her which she kept in the Bentley for similar situations. There was little talk between the two as they took the elevator up to their floor. As the door opened they both looked up and down the corridor making sure it was empty.

Austin opened the door to his suite. It had two large bedrooms which shared one huge ornate bath, and as Hannah headed for it Austin thought he would tease her.

He asked her, as she paused with her hand on the door, "What do you wear to bed?" He thought the answer would embarrass her.

Hannah smiled a sweet, mischievous grin, "Chanel Number 5!"

She giggled at the shocked expression on Austin's face, and softly slammed the door.

Austin stood staring at the closed bathroom door as he fought the images coming into his lascivious male mind, until he finally walked away muttering to himself. "Nah, she is just putting me on!"

Hannah looked around the bathroom and marveled at Austin's neatness even in a hotel. His razor, soap cup, and brush were all laid out perfectly straight. His toothbrush was in a water glass on one side of the sink. His hand towel was folded on the other side of the sink and his comb and brush lay on top in perfect order.

"I just thought I was neat," Hannah said to herself.

After a hot shower she dressed in flannel pajamas. Hannah eased into bed and was asleep before she could do more than smile to herself about what Austin could be thinking in the next room. She slept soundly for she knew she was safe for the first time in a long while.

The room was starting to lighten from the impending sunrise as Hannah awoke. She lay in bed wondering if Austin needed the bathroom first. Her thought was answered when she heard the water running in the sink as Austin shaved and then brushed his teeth. He showered quickly, wrapped a heavy robe around his body, and knocked softly on the door from the bathroom to her bedroom; he knew she was awake. She pulled the covers up under her chin, and answered, "Yes?"

Austin said with a smile in his voice, "The bathroom is yours. I will order up breakfast, tea for you and coffee for me. Poached eggs and croissants okay?"

"Yes, that will be fine."

She heard him shut the door to his bedroom loud enough for her to hear. When she heard him on the telephone ordering room service, she crept out of bed and into the bathroom. She locked the door and looked again at how neat Austin left the place. She smiled and shook her head to think a man kept house like him. "Where have you been all my life?" She wondered to herself; then blushed at the thought. .Hurriedly she showered, dressed, did her hair, and put on a little lipstick. She was ready for work.

The breakfast order came and Austin

tipped and thanked the man.

"No! Thank you!" the man was polite and very appreciative of the generous tip.

After they ate Austin stacked the dishes and folded the napkins causing Hannah to smile a small smile and shake her head to herself. Austin obviously thought it was proper to share in keeping house. He opened the door slowly, and after he assured himself the corridor was empty, he pushed the table into the hall and next to the room two doors down.

The twosome took a cab instead of calling for the Bentley, and getting out of a cab together raised a few eyebrows but no one said anything. Clandestine couples happened often in their line of work.

Ignoring the attention from Hannah's coworkers of Austin sitting in her office, Austin with a serious look on his face asked, "What now? The KGB knows a lot about when and where we come and go. They are stalking both of us, but I have a suggestion. Let's both go for a two week vacation to the United States. I have not been home in two years, and with Christmas coming up next week we could surprise everybody."

Hannah shrugged her shoulders, "I don't know, Austin," she began.

"Separate bedrooms, of course." He smiled.

"That is not it. Logistically I would be out of the office if anything happened."

"We have phones in Alabama, and my brother-in law and cousin who live in my house have a short wave radio if the office needed us in a hurry."

"I appreciate the invitation, but why don't you go by yourself and visit your family?"

"You're right. I am just worried a little about you being by yourself and me not here to protect you."

"Trust me, Austin. Look around. I have plenty of people looking out for me. I appreciate the macho attitude, but you will have your own hands full if he comes looking for you."

"At least it will be on my own turf. He can't hide in Birmingham as easy as he does here. Any kind of accent is suspicious in the South if they don't say yall." He smiled.

"Go by and see if we have something to help you in the way of hidden ordnance if he does find you."

After taking most of what was available, Austin had a briefcase with a knife and a small caliber pistol hidden inside, an exploding ink pen, and he took a hidden pistol to put on his leg. He showed it all to Hannah. "I am only taking on one or two men, you know, and I am going to be so over laden with equipment I can't use martial arts."

"Quit fussing," smiled an unsympathetic

Hannah. "It may interest you to know most of this is standard service issue for the people in our field. The double O's are laden with even more. Besides, I want you to come back." Her voice softened and Austin knew what she meant.

Home Again

The big, four engine plane touched down on the tarmac runway in Birmingham with barely a squeak from the tires.

"Not bad flying," Austin said to himself.

He took his suit bag, suitcase, and briefcase from the overhead. He walked out of the plane, down the steps, and into the terminal.

"Austin!" shouted a familiar voice. He turned to see Anna Lee and Fred running to meet him. Fred was smiling and after the embraces and handshakes they went out of the terminal arm in arm.

Fred's new car was an Oldsmobile sedan, and when Austin questioned him about it, he shrugged his shoulders and smiled.

"Anna says we have to grow up sometime and put away boyish toys."

"But an Oldsmobile? My dad owns an

Oldsmobile. Next thing she will be making you wear a suit and tie when you go out and eat!"

Austin burst into laughter when they looked at each other.

"What can I say?" smiled Fred.

As the car slowed to pull into the driveway, Austin had a grim flashback to another time when he came home from the war. He was quiet for he could still hear his wife and the servants celebrating his return. This time was not so much fun, even though Samuel and the girls tried. Austin held them all close while the girls cried. Anna was amazed and saddened when Austin showed very little emotion.

Later, after a huge meal, while Samuel and the girls cleaned the kitchen, Anna, Fred, and Austin sat in the library and visited around the fire.

"What cars do we have left?" asked Austin.

"Believe it or not, we still have the Duesenberg and your '40 Ford convertible. You loved those cars so much we just could not sell them. However, the Duesenberg will already bring several times the original price. Your Ford is being used as a hot rod by the teenagers now and could be sold too."

"Really?" asked Austin visibly excited. "I will drive one of them over to Little Rock for Christmas. I may want to stay a few days with the folks."

Samuel had kept both cars impeccable for which Austin shook his hand and patted him. Austin took the Duesenberg for a short drive to check it out, and then packed a suitcase and a garment bag which he loaded into the back. He left about ten o' clock, and after a six hour trip on the new highways at not always the speed limit, Austin pulled into the driveway of his parents' home. The house and grounds were already brightly decorated for Christmas.

The sound of Austin's car in the driveway, and his signature horn hello, brought everyone outside to greet him. There were embraces and tears everywhere. For the first time in a long while, Austin smiled and laughed. It was good to be home

Mallory

After a boring morning the third day he was home, Austin drove the Duesenberg into downtown Little Rock. He had heard Dillard's Department Store installed an escalator, and he wanted to see and ride it. He parked the car in a secure place and walked the block to the store. He had forgotten how America was on show in department store windows. He was interested and amazed after Europe the past few years which was still rebuilding from the devastation of the war.

At Dillard's he stood in front of the window by the front entrance, which displayed men's fashions. A beautiful blonde woman walked out and was trying to free her arm from the grip of a well-dressed man.

"Leave me alone, creep!"

"Aw come on, baby. Let me buy you a drink!"

"I don't want a drink, and I don't want to be seen with you!" She jerked her arm free, and when the man reached for her again his wrist was caught in the powerful grip of Austin.

"I think the lady has made her point, sonny boy. Why don't you run along while you still can?" said Austin evenly.

He let go and the man rubbed his arm. The look in Austin's eyes made him hesitate for a moment. The guys he had been used to bullying were mostly college kids, but this man did not look afraid of him in the least. He tried to bluff his way with tough talk.

"Who do you think you are, Bucko?" the man asked. "I oughta give you a beating for just touching me."

"That would give me a lot of pleasure, friend, to just have you try."

He stepped toward Austin, and before he could put his hands up, Austin grabbed him by the nose between his thumb and forefinger and bent him to his knees.

"Oh, Oh, Oh, that hurts! Let go!"

Austin applied a little more pressure. "We are through here, right? Nod your head if you agree!"

The man's eyes began to water, and the pain in his nose was so unbearable it was nearly causing him to lose consciousness. He realized he was caught, and he nodded his head up and down. He started to get up as Austin let go, but thought he might better wait for further instructions. He stayed on his knees.

"Who are you?"

"My name is Austin Johnson, and you owe this young lady an apology."

"Austin! Is that really you?" exclaimed the woman. She grabbed him with her arms around him, and put her head on his chest and began to cry.

Austin let her cry for a few seconds as he realized he knew her. It was Mallory Potter, his girlfriend from high school! He took out his handkerchief and wiped her eyes tenderly as she took a sobbing breath. "Oh Austin, I have thought about you every day for years! I can't believe it is finally you!"

"Sir?" The man on his knees asked politely. "I am sorry for the trouble. May I please go now?"

The small crowd that had gathered laughed at him.

"What do you think, Mallory? Has he had enough for now? Tell you what. You apologize to Mallory and tell her you will never come near her without her permission. Have I made myself clear? Next time I will hurt you. Go ahead, apologize, and then get out of here!"

"Yes, sir! I will, sir!" He looked at Mallory so pitifully that she hid her smile with her hand.

"Just go, Seymour."

The man stood carefully to his feet and did not take his eyes from Austin. He turned his back and took off at a run, as the crowd laughed and jeered.

"Austin, what are you doing here? I thought you were in Britain."

"I came home for a Christmas visit."

They walked arm in arm into the store and Austin hesitated at the escalator. She laughed and pulled him onto the moving walk. Austin caught his balance quickly and stepped up beside Mallory as they were carried up. They got off on the top floor where there was a nice restaurant.

"I could use a drink, how about you, Austin?"

"Sure."

Mallory held his hand across the table and looked at him. She saw he was now a man, not the kid with the swagger she knew from high school.

He still made her heart flutter like no one else.

Austin smiled at her for a moment and then said, "The family told me about Benny. I am sorry for your loss. Do you want to talk?"

"It has been some time now. He came back from the war wounded, picked up the bottle, and never sat it back down. We divorced about three years ago, while you were in Alabama. Not more than a couple of months later he shot himself. I had a lot of guilt, but even though I loved him, I could not help him. It was so sad."

"So what are you up to now?"

"Well, Benny left me a lot of money and a nice home. I am okay there. I have gone back to church and I have a lot of good support from everyone. Your brother James and my sister Payton live next door and we eat together nearly every day. I think I am great. I am on my own for the first time in my life, and until I saw you I was not lonely. Don't leave soon, Austin. Please?" Her hands held his tightly, and her eyes filled with tears. He held her hands with his hand over hers and he was filled with all sorts of emotions.

"Don't start to cry again. I only had one handkerchief!" They both laughed.

"Can I give you a ride home?" asked Austin.

"Sure. Let me tell Payton to go on home when she gets off. She was wrapping presents here at Dillard's."

Austin and Mallory went by to tell Payton and she was glad to see Austin. The smile on Mallory's face was a comfort for her sister after such a long time seeing her sad.

As they drove along the river, Austin asked, "I have not seen any submarine races since you and I watched way back in '42. Want to see them again?" He parked in an empty paved viewing area, and turned off the engine and lights.

Mallory looked at him for a long moment before she answered, "Yes. It would be nice to feel your arms around me again. You know I have loved you all these years, don't you? Even being married to someone else for a while has not changed anything. Austin, I know what you and your wife had was good, and I respect that. I will wait and when you are ready, I will be here."

Austin just held her without saying a word for a moment then spoke softly, "Mallory, it has been just two and a half years since my wife was shot. While it could be possible for us, I have unfinished business with her killer and I do not want you part of that, okay?"

Mallory nodded yes and put her head on his chest, and was satisfied for the moment to know he cared about her.

Austin believed it might be a good thing to be seen all over town. He hoped if there were an assassin about, it might bring him out.

Austin went by and reacquainted himself with the Police Chief. When he told him he was going to act like a playboy to draw the suspect out. The chief thought it would be a good thing, but he warned him, "Please don't have a shoot out in a public place. I don't want a bunch of dead bodies to have to deal with."

Austin smiled a slight smile. "I want it to be just him and me. I hope he is here. If I want to go back to Britain all this will be settled."

"So you may be going back. Does Mallory know?"

"No, and please do not tell her anything. I have a lot to settle here before I would go. For now could I have a temporary assignment as an undercover investigator? I am trained you know."

"Sure. Start when you are ready. Pretty quiet now the war is over, but I do need help training my guys in the latest equipment."

The pair shook hands with the bonds of a

long time friendship

Austin and Mallory drew tremendous attention whenever they were seen in public. The newspaper carried the story of the "Millionaire Playboy War Hero and the Millionaire Socialite." Pictures were taken every time they sat or walked into a club or restaurant.

Austin had been back in Little Rock only a few weeks, and on New Year's Eve the phone rang late at night. It was a long distance call from London.

"Well, well, are you having a good time?" Hannah smiled into the phone. She did not want Austin to know she missed him.

"What do you think? I am trying to find a hit man, but until I do, this is covering up my anxiety."

"Oh, of course, Austin. Your picture in the newspaper at the Country Club with a beautiful blonde all smiles and hanging on your arm looks like you forgot your anxiety and what you went home to find."

Hannah's tone was a little sharper than she meant to be. Austin's laugh did not help.

"Do you miss me even a little?" Austin asked.

"Not in the least." She lied. "Okay, maybe a little when I need the dishes washed."

"There you go. I miss your smile, Hannah. Happy New Year! I wish we were under the mistletoe!"

She softened for she knew he did think of her too. She told him they had information from the underground someone was already in Birmingham to take him out.

"Thanks, and I am very aware of my surroundings all the time. You be safe too, my friend. This is not just about me you know. If the SS could get to you it would give them a lot of credibility."

After Austin hung up, a few moments passed as Hannah thought of Austin and stared at the phone. Finally the sadness went away enough to hang up the phone and sever the connection to him. With a shock she realized she was in love with him.

David Duke

A few days after New Year's, Austin went shopping by himself for Mallory a birthday present. He watched the crowd around him to see if he was being followed, and he did not see anyone who seemed to pay any undue attention to him.

He rode the escalator to the 3rd floor where the public restrooms were located. He went into one of the stalls and crouched on top of a commode where no one could see his feet. After a few minutes the door opened slowly and he could hear footsteps quietly checking under each stall. When the footsteps stopped in front of his stall, he kicked the door open. He caught the man by surprise and he bounced off the wall. Austin pulled his pistol and aimed at the man's midsection.

"You looking for me?"

"Are you Austin Johnson?"

"Maybe. Who's asking and why?"

"My name is David Duke from British Intelligence. You should remember me as Hannah's part time driver. Hannah sent me to help you and guard you. I took a cab and followed you from your home."

"Let's see some ID."

His identification looked authentic to Austin, but he did not lower the gun.

"What is Hannah's middle name?" asked Austin.

"Why, I don't know. She is the director and she is very private."

"I don't know either," smiled Austin, and lowered the gun. The man let out the breath he had been holding. Austin put his Beretta away in the shoulder holster under his coat. Austin put out his hand to shake with the man.

"I figured if you tried to lie and gave me a

fictitious name you would have been a hit man. I would have shot you. Don't ever lie to me."

"Don't worry. I won't. I believe you would shoot me or anyone else if you had a good reason. Can we get out of this rest room and find a place with a little more ambience? I need a drink after all that."

The Plan

David took a sip of his martini and sat it down. He sat up straight and looked at Austin. "What do you want me to do?"

"Hannah said there is someone already here. Watch my back and as much of my family as you can. He knows where I live and more I am afraid. I do not want to lose anyone else. Try to stay out of sight."

"Fair enough. You may not see me, but I have your back."

"What disguise will you use?"

"I am somewhat hampered with my accent, but I pass easy enough as a tourist or a visitor from Britain."

"Come with me to my home and I will introduce you to the staff and my family as an old friend from Britain. I will take you by and introduce you also to Chief Howard. He is a friend, and he will be comforted to know I have a little back up."

Austin introduced David Duke to his family after he took him by the police station. Everyone was glad Austin had help if he needed it. David moved into a spare bedroom and followed Austin when they went out in an extra car, which Austin kept on hand for visitors.

Bruno

Bruno Gruber turned off the car lights and pulled onto the grassy shoulder of the road a few yards before the driveway leading into the Johnson Estate. He smiled to not find a gate or a guard even though the brick columns were huge. They supported a wrought iron sign over the drive that simply said, Johnson.

He looked and listened for a watch dog, and, found nothing but a darkened drive which led to the house which sat peaceful in the night. He walked through the gate. His rubber soled shoes made a slight crunch sound, but after a pause to listen, he walked a few steps more and then onto the stone walk. He walked without a sound.

Austin awakened with a start, and as he lay in the darkness whatever he had heard he did not like. The sound was not normal. After all the sleepless nights he had spent, it did not belong. He eased his .45 from under the pillow and crept to the corner of the stairs to be able to see the front door. The knob turned slightly. The door was locked, and whoever it was walked silently around the house toward the pool. Austin went down the side stairs from his room which led into the kitchen. He stood in the darkened doorway. A man came crashing through the plate glass door. It was Gruber and he had been shot, and as he raised his pistol, Austin shouted, "Freeze!"

Gruber chose to end his life with a turn toward Austin. He was shot in the chest twice and he was dead before he fell back onto the tiled kitchen floor.

Austin turned the lights on and David stood in the ruined glass door with his pistol drawn and still smoking. Fred came into the room also with a gun.

"What are you doing up?" Austin asked Fred.

"I looked out the window while I rocked the baby to sleep, and I happened to see a car pull off the road a short distance from the entrance. I put the baby down in her crib and grabbed my pistol. I figured it was Gruber or someone who did not want us to see him. It turned out I was right."

"Go back to the baby. Have Anna call Chief Howard, and David and I will go check out the car."

By the time the police arrived, the two determined Gruber had been driving the car and it was probably stolen. In a thorough investigation of the interior, Austin and Fred found no prints or evidence in the car, and they were going through Gruber's pockets when the police arrived with lights flashing but no sirens.

David went to direct the police. Austin found a business card from a local nightclub, Rosie's, with the name Jeanette and a phone number on the back in the dead man's bloody shirt pocket. Gruber had a passport from Argentina and twelve hundred American dollars.

"International spying must not be paying as well as when your brother was alive and active. He had three thousand in his wallet at a time when that was a lot of money," Austin whispered to the corpse and pocketed the money, business card, and passport.

The sensational shooting made headlines in the local newspapers. It was picked up by the wire services and went nationwide on radio. Austin was interviewed several times during the next couple of days being a local war hero.

Two nights later he and David sat and discussed the events when the phone rang. It was next to Austin and he answered.

"Are you okay?" asked a very concerned Hannah.

"No hello? I love you? How's your mother?"

"I am sorry. I am worried about your well being."

"Of course I am okay. David shot the guy, but I got all the credit. Thanks for sending backup."

After the assurance he was not harmed, Hannah asked, "What's next for you, Austin?"

"I'll take some time and sort through some things. I'll go ahead and send David home if he wants to come. Hopefully the drama is over. The police force could use me here and I will stay a while. Put me on leave for a few months. I need to help the Chief set up labs for the identification of suspects."

Hannah was let down more than she thought she might be. She was quiet for a moment.

"Are you still there?"

"Yes."

David and Mallory

Austin decided to hire Mallory to be a secretary at his office, but was unprepared for the attention she received. David seemed to hang out in his office a lot more than usual, and the other detectives seemed to have a lot more questions than ever before that needed his personal attention. They talked to him but they looked at Mallory if she was in the room.

Austin began to second guess her hiring, but she was a competent secretary. He knew he could trust her. She was used to attention and knew how to keep the men at arm's length. Being easy on the eyes did not hurt, and she dressed very professionally. The only time she seemed to make eye contact with any man except Austin was when David was in the room.

At first, Austin did not pay much attention, but one day Mallory handed David a stack of papers and let her hand linger for a moment on the back of his. Austin smiled to himself as David reddened.

"Must be tough to concentrate with her flirting," thought Austin. "It is a good thing he is British and keeps himself under tight control at all times."

There were times, however, when she had to stand close to him to share a paper or an item of interest, and Austin thought he saw his hands shake.

"Austin, may I speak with you?" asked David one afternoon from the open doorway.

"Sure. Come in and have a seat. What's on your mind?"

David looked down for a moment as if embarrassed, and sat before he answered.

Austin shut the door of his office to help keep things private.

"We are friends as well as coworkers,

wouldn't you say?"

"Yes, I would."

"Is there a rule about coworkers dating?"

"Yes. There is."

He looked at David for a moment and grinned. "It has to be a male and a female."

David instantly brightened. "Ah, well. I assure you that is the case." He smiled and began to speak with excited animation. They discussed the Gruber shooting and the business card Austin found from Rosie's nightclub. It had the name Jeanette and a phone number on the back, and Austin decided to not tell anyone except David and Chief Howard.

"I have been watching you and Mallory, and you are a lucky man, David. I warn you though; she is a lot of woman with a mind of her own."

"Then, is it okay if we go out to dinner or a nightclub or something?"

"Of course, but how does Mallory feel?"

"We are to go out the first time tonight. In fact I will be giving her a ride home."

"Man. I didn't know you Brits moved that quickly."

"Well, the truth is, Mallory asked me for a ride home, and she said yes when I asked could I take her out someplace nice to eat."

"There you go, old friend. Have fun. Can you dance? She loves to dance."

"I love to dance. We have great night clubs in England you know."

"Sounds like a match made in Heaven to me. Take her to Rosie's tonight and I will meet you two there at nine. I will call Michael, the concierge, for a reservation for three close to the dance floor. I will come alone in my car. Maybe I can find out who Jeanette is and what she has to do with Bruno."

Jeanette

At five minutes to nine, Austin idled the Duesenberg into the valet line. There was an instant buzz and interest about the car and who might be driving. Two valets hurried to the car. One opened the door and the other undid the velvet rope in the celebrity space close to the front entrance. Austin parked the car and handed the man the keys and two 50 dollar bills.

"No one touches the car, right?"

"Yes sir, Mr. Johnson."

He smiled at the two valets, and as he started up the steps into the club Mallory and David were waiting.

"So much for a mundane entrance, Austin. Every person in the place will know you are here!"

"That is the point. I am hoping someone named Jeanette will notice."

The concierge personally escorted the

threesome to a table for four on the edge of the dance floor. With a snap of his fingers, menus and setups appeared almost instantly.

Austin smiled at Mallory for he knew she was impressed by the attention afforded him and the group. She smiled back and nodded at him in appreciation.

She was part of the social event of the evening, even though she happened to be with someone else. She reminded herself of the date with David, but had no problem reaching over to hold his hand. David turned to look at her at the touch and smiled.

"Do you think anyone even knows we are here?"

"It is no big thing, David. It happens every time I am with Austin. I have gotten used to it."

The drinks had just been served when a beautiful, brown-eyed woman with raven black hair approached the table. The men stood and

Austin offered her a chair by him. She smiled and spoke with a trace of a European accent.

"I am Jeanette. I was told there was a good-looking rich guy asking to meet me. Well, here I am."

Only Austin Johnson would have been able to maintain his composure, after such a statement from the most beautiful woman he had ever seen.

Before he sat, Austin smiled, put out his hand to shake and said, "If I am not, I hope you can make do with me until we find him."

The lady smiled back warmly as she looked him up and down. "You'll do, handsome."

Austin saw even Mallory was silently in awe of this woman who had the obvious class, the beauty, and the offhand nonchalance to handle the stares of every person in the place.

Jeanette put her hand on Austin's forearm. Even through his dinner jacket and dress shirt, he could feel the heat.

"Now what could a man like you want with a little girl like me?"

There were a number of scenarios that passed through Austin's mind, but he smiled and said, "For now how about a dance?"

Austin stood and offered his hand. Jeanette was used to men similar in style to Austin, but she was impressed by him. She did not sense any fluff or nonsense. By the time he guided her to the floor, she decided she would wait and see what he wanted. She knew enough about men to appreciate the real thing. Men like Austin did not stay in her life for long. For the moment she would enjoy their time together.

The band had finished a song, and Norm, the band leader and an old friend, motioned for Austin to request a song. He sent word by a waiter for him to sing the love song, Unforgettable. Norm smiled as he nodded his approval.

At the first romantic strains of the music,

Austin stood and whirled Jeanette around and held her close. She was surprised he was such an accomplished dancer. The floor was nearly devoid of others as they left it to let the couple dance. When the song ended, Austin bowed to Jeanette and to Norm. The room erupted in applause.

He escorted Jeanette to their table and Austin asked, "Is there somewhere we could go and talk?"

"You know I have to sing at least one more song, don't you?"

"No problem. I'll wait."

After she sang, the couple walked outside. Austin saw Jeanette was impressed to be receiving a ride in a Duesenberg. He could tell her opinion of him was growing by the moment.

The couple parked by the river in an observation spot, and listened silently to a song by Frank Sinatra on the radio. She knew Austin was more of a man than to take a girl parking. He wanted to talk. If he had wanted anything more he would have tried to take her to a hotel.

"What's on your mind, Austin?"

With no hesitation Austin asked, "Why would a woman like you give her name and phone number to a snake like Gruber?"

She was taken by surprise. "How did you know about it, and why would it matter to you? I heard he was shot a few nights ago. He was a very persistent man; the type I run across from time to time. He was stalking me and kept popping up nearly every time I went out."

She looked him in the eyes and whispered, "You are the one who shot him, aren't you? Thank you for freeing me from that man. I knew you were something more than a lounge lizard! Do I want to know who you are? Am I putting my life in danger?"

Austin ignored her question. "Why was the handwriting on the card yours?"

"Austin, you can check this out. A few nights ago I did give the card to a nice, rich, middle-aged man and Bruno must have seen. The man was found in his car shot to death in an alley the next morning. When the card was not mentioned, I knew who did it. But, I have my own life to protect, and I knew better than to tell the police."

"Good girl," smiled Austin. He put his arms around her, drew her to him, and she did not hesitate to kiss him long and well. Both were breathing heavily as they broke the kiss. She laid her head on his shoulder.

"You are quite a man, Austin."

"Why the tears then?"

He took his pocket handkerchief and tenderly dabbed at her cheeks.

"Because I know you are going to take me home, kiss me goodnight outside my door, and I will probably never see you again. I don't know what I am doing wrong to not be able to attract and keep a man like you. Someone beat me to it, didn't they? She is a lucky woman, Austin."

"Jeanette, Bruno is dead. He was one masher that you will no longer have to deal with. I hope it is a consolation you have a friend in me if it ever occurs again. It is sometimes a curse to be beautiful and talented. The good men are intimidated, and the powerful rich men want to use you or have you for another pretty trinket to wear on their arm."

"So, what do I do?"

Austin dried the tears on her cheeks with his handkerchief. He held her close as she looked up with her head on his chest. He whispered, "Enjoy moments like this with men you can trust."

"Austin, if the other woman and you do not work out, promise you'll come back to me."

At the door of her upscale apartment, Austin drew her close, kissed her, and let go.

Hannah

Hannah was at her desk. Aimlessly she moved papers from one pile to another. Staring out the window at a dreary, rainy day did not help her restlessness. David Duke had resigned and decided to stay in the USA. She was upset Austin had not called if he indeed was going to resign.

The secretary, in an uncommon move, got up from her chair and came into Hannah's office and said in an urgent low voice, "Incoming call for the director."

"Who is it?"

"He would not say, but said it was very important, and he did not want to be put on eternal hold! He is very emphatic!"

Irritated, Hannah picked up her phone thinking it was some bureaucrat. Before she punched the hold button, she frowned, and waved off her secretary by pointing to her and then to her office. The woman did not go quickly or far.

"This is the director. How may I help you?"

A familiar voice said, "I need a lunch date and I was wondering, would you be free this morning?"

The End